TRACK OF

THE BEAST

A BROCK STONE ADVENTURE

DAVID WOOD

ADRENALINE PRESS

Track of the Beast-Author's Preferred Edition ©2022, 2021 by David Wood

Published by Adrenaline Press
www.adrenaline.press

Adrenaline Press is an imprint of Gryphonwood Press
www.gryphonwoodpress.com

Edited by Melissa Bowersock

Cover art by Drazenka Kimpel

ISBN: 978-1-950920-32-7

BOOKS BY DAVID WOOD

Devil's Face
Herald
Brainwash
The Tomb
Shasta
Legends
Golden Dragon
Emerald Dragon
Baal (forthcoming)
Destination: Rio
Destination: Luxor
Destination: Sofia

Bones Bonebrake Adventures
Primitive
The Book of Bones
Skin and Bones
Venom

Brock Stone Adventures
Arena of Souls
Track of the Beast
Curse of the Pharaoh (forthcoming)

Jade Ihara Adventures (with Sean Ellis)
Oracle
Changeling
Exile

Myrmidon Files with Sean Ellis
Destiny
Mystic

Jake Crowley Adventures (with Alan Baxter)
Sanctum
Blood Codex

Anubis Key
Revenant

Sam Aston Investigations (with Alan Baxter)
Primordial
Overlord
Crocalypse

Stand-Alone Novels
Into the Woods (with David S. Wood)
The Zombie-Driven Life
You Suck
Callsign: Queen (with Jeremy Robinson)
Dark Rite (with Alan Baxter)

Writing as Finn Gray
Aquaria Falling
Aquaria Burning
The Gate

Writing as David Debord

The Absent Gods Trilogy
The Silver Serpent
Keeper of the Mists
The Gates of Iron

The Impostor Prince (with Ryan A. Span)
Neptune's Key

FROM THE AUTHOR

Several years back, I took on the challenge of writing an old-school pulp adventure in the spirit of Doc Savage and other classic adventure stories, and the Brock Stone Adventures were born. The first book, *Arena of Souls*, was written as a weekly serial with no plan. Every week, I sat down and wrote a chapter. The end result was a fun story, but looking back, I can tell that I didn't yet have a handle on the characters or the tone of the series.

With *Track of the Beast*, I've tried to lean into the things I love about writing Dane Maddock—mystery, history, monsters, conspiracies, adventure, and humor. Even if *Arena of Souls* was not your cup of tea, if you enjoy my other adventure novels, I think you will *love Track of the Beast!*

In this Author's Preferred Edition, we begin exploring Stone's mysterious past by way of a "flashback" story woven into the narrative.

Thank you and happy reading!
David

TRACK OF THE BEAST

Original concept sketch by Drazenka Kimpel.

1– SHADOWS IN THE DARK

"One more drink before I hit the road." Sam Price raised his empty mug, as if Wayne, the bartender, needed the illustration to go along with his request. He let out a loud belch and patted his gut. He felt the beginning of a paunch. Logging was hard work, but Sam was thirty-five, and Lord knew he consumed enough beer and slugburgers. There was nothing else to do in these parts, so why not?

"You sure can put them away." Wayne, a burly man with pale skin and black hair. slid the mug across the rough wooden surface of the bar, foam spilling over the lip and onto Sam's hand.

"Hey, careful now. I paid for the whole drink." Sam grinned.

"You gonna turn me in?" Wayne replied. He was a reserved sort and it was always hard to tell when he was joking.

"Of course not." Establishments like these were technically illegal. Most speakeasys pretended to be a different sort of business. Here in the mountains of the Pacific Northwest, no one bothered to pretend. The revenue man assigned to this area dropped by a couple times a year to accept his bribe and enjoy a few drinks, all the while bemoaning the fact that prohibition would probably come to an end soon.

Sam turned on his stool and looked around the joint. The Woodsman's Complaint was a dark, dreary place. Most of the light came from the roaring fireplace. It was late summer, but it got cold after sundown. Only a couple of patrons remained, nursing their beers and puffing on pipes or hand-rolled cigarettes. A blue haze surrounded them, and the whole place reeked of smoke and spilled beer. Even if there were any eligible women around, they wouldn't be caught dead in a place like this.

Discouraged, Sam drained his beer, left a few coins on the bar, and staggered toward the door.

"Time to make tracks," he announced to anyone who might be listening.

"You going to make it all right?" Wayne asked with a touch of indifference.

"Abyssinia!" Sam had picked up the slang term for farewell on a brief visit to New York City. So far it had not caught on in these parts, but he was trying. Not looking back, Sam waved and headed out into the night. The crisp air did not exactly sharpen his senses, but he felt a touch more alert now that he was out of the cramped, smoky bar.

He spared a minute to take a leak against the side of the bar, barely managing to keep his boots clean, and then began the long walk back to camp.

The moon was out, painting the dirt road in a light brushing of silver. As he moved deeper into the forest, though, the way grew dark, with barely enough light to keep from losing his way.

He didn't care. He could make this trek with his eyes closed. He was tempted to try it, but if he closed his eyes, he'd probably fall asleep. He shouldn't have stayed out so late or drank so much. He would pay for it tomorrow.

He quickened his pace, lengthened his stride, and hurried on. As he moved along, the scant light melted away as dark clouds drifted over the moon.

"Guess I'll get to test my theory after all." He spoke louder than absolutely necessary, the sound of his own voice emboldening him. He was a woodsman, plenty rugged, but being unable to see more than a few feet in front of his face unnerved him.

He remembered sitting on the front porch of his childhood home in southwest Virginia, listening to his grandfather tell stories of witches and haints, the ghosts that haunted the Blue Ridge Mountains. He didn't believe those stories, at least, not most of the time, but when he was alone in the dark, they suddenly seemed just a touch more plausible.

Sam Price, how did you ever end up over here on the wrong side of the country? he thought. It was an unexpected turn of events. With his hometown caught in the grip of the Great Depression, he had traveled all the way to New York City looking for work, and ended up in Washington of all places. But, the job kept him fed, clothed, and sheltered, with a little left over to send home. Minus drinking money, of course. Still, these mountains had a different feel to those back East. Sometimes he felt like he had traveled to an alien world.

It wasn't long before he heard it. A single crunch, as if someone who had been moving silently had made a single misstep. Sam froze, listened. Nothing.

He started moving again, ears straining to hear something over the sound of his labored breathing and racing heart.

There it was again. Something was definitely moving.

"Could be anything. Deer, squirrel, wolf. Nothing that'll give you any trouble." Despite his feigned confidence, he unsheathed his Bowie knife and clutched it tightly.

He continued on, wondering just how much farther it was to camp. The darkness and his alcohol-polluted mind had deprived him of his senses of time and distance. If he was close to camp, maybe it was one of the fellows out wandering in the forest for some reason of his own. Yes! That made sense.

"Anybody out there?" he called.

Five seconds of heart-pounding silence. And then the footsteps came again, this time from both sides of the road.

"Who the hell is following me?" He wished he didn't sound so fearful. "It's late and I don't have time for your jokes. Come on out."

And then a new sound came. A sharp, rapping sound, like someone knocking two sticks together. He turned in the direction of the sound. It came again.

"Oh, my God." He'd heard the stories, knew what it meant. Had he taken a wrong turn?

Like a band tuning up for a show, the sounds now came from several directions, up ahead and off to his left. Sharp staccatos and deep thrums, like someone pounding a tree.

They're up in front of me, but I am sure camp is that way. What do I do?

Suddenly, his knife seemed a pitiful weapon against whoever was out there.

Where do I go? Can I even outrun them?

His cognitive processes suddenly gummed up and his hindbrain took over. He spun on his heel and dashed blindly back through the darkness. He'd go back to town and sleep it off in the bar, assuming Wayne would let him. Hell, even if he couldn't find a place to stay, he'd rather sleep in the street than stay in this forest a moment longer than necessary.

He was just getting up a full head of steam when something large and heavy smacked him full in the face. A flash of red light filled his eyes and a loud pop echoed in his ears.

Stunned, he stumbled backward and sat down heavily on the soft, damp earth. His eyes watered, his ears rang, and his nose felt like it had been burned with a hot poker. He put his hands to his face and felt warm blood.

"What hit me?" he groaned.

Suddenly afraid, he kicked out in the direction of whatever had struck him, and his foot connected with something solid. He let out a fresh grunt as pain blossomed in his ankle. He had run full tilt into a tree.

"Jesus Christ and all His disciples. What is wrong with me?" He staggered to his feet, squeezed one nostril closed, and took a deep breath. Just in time, he remembered something he'd learned years ago. *Don't try to blow your nose if you think it's broken. Your eyes will puff up like balloons.*

He settled for wiping the blood with the back of his sleeve. As he recovered from the stunning blow, he suddenly remembered the reason he had been running in the first place.

The clacking sounds continued. He realized he'd dropped his knife. He felt around with his foot for a few seconds, but gave up. The sounds were coming closer.

And then, despite his bloody, broken nose, he caught a whiff of something foul. It was feral, almost like the foul odor of a polecat.

"Lord have mercy! It's true. It's all true."

He took off running again. He kept his hands out in front of him this time, hoping to avoid any further collisions. It took only a few moments to realize he had left the road. Here, the ground was uneven beneath his feet. Leaves crackled and crunched underfoot, low-hanging limbs smacked him. He was running blind, no idea where he was headed, but at least he was still running.

Twice he stumbled and fell, the second time getting a mouthful of dirt for his trouble. Cursing, he pushed himself up to his knees, spitting out soil and bits of leaves and twigs.

It was then that two things happened.

The foul stench grew overwhelming, and the moon broke free of the clouds.

Sam looked up and gasped.

Standing in front of him was the dark outline of something huge.

He didn't have time to scream before everything went black.

2— THE PYRAMID

The morning sun shone down on the pyramid that stood just up ahead. Brock Stone parted the foliage to gain a better look. The structure was built in the four-sided Egyptian style and made of granite. Like its Middle Eastern counterparts, it lacked a smooth outer surface. In the case of the Great Pyramids of Egypt, those had once been covered in polished limestone, all of which had been looted over the years, leaving the foundation blocks exposed. Stone knew that this pyramid, however, had not had such an outer covering.

"I can't believe there is an actual pyramid here." A tall, red-haired man was peering through binoculars at the object in the distance. He was lanky, his fair skin sunburned and scraped. His left arm ended in a modified hook attached to the stump of his wrist, and it was in this hook that he clutched the binoculars. "It's just so out of place." A friend from Stone's youth, Alex English was his closest friend.

Stone shrugged. "That's what makes it interesting. That, and it's in the correct general location. We should investigate. Come on."

"You do realize you're not Percy Fawcett exploring the Amazon? It's 1932 and this is Virginia." Alex heaved a tired sigh. "And that is a long walk."

"It's a much longer walk home," Stone said. "And if you abandon me now, I promise I won't give you a lift back."

"You've got a heart of stone, Brock."

"That joke gets funnier every time you tell it. Let's go." Stone pushed his way through the thick tangle of shrubs and tree branches and stepped out into an open field. The tall grass was wet with morning dew, and the air was crisp and cool. Another beautiful Virginia morning.

"Tell me again how a pyramid came to be built in northern Virginia," Alex said, falling into step with his friend. The two made an odd pair. Stone was tall, tan, and muscular, with brown hair and eyes. Alex was even taller, skinny and pale with flame-red hair and green eyes.

"In 1897 the Confederate Memorial Literary Society requested that Virginia railroad executives erect markers at spots of historical significance."

"Why?" Alex asked.

"Depends on who you ask. Most say it was to give passengers something to look at. Others say it was part of a conspiracy."

"What sort of conspiracy?"

"That part is a mystery," Stone said.

They crossed a set of railroad tracks and proceeded up a gentle slope.

"If they wanted the passengers to admire the pyramid, why did they build it all the way up there?" Alex asked.

"Another mystery, and part of the reason I want to give it a closer look."

"You think it's connected to John Kane?" Alex asked.

John Kane was a New York City businessman whose dealings were cloaked beneath a shroud of intrigue. When Stone had returned to America to claim his inheritance and resume civilian life, Kane's hired thugs had made attempts on Stone's life. They had continued to dog his steps as he and his friends ventured into a place some sailors called the Devil's Triangle, a mysterious and deadly patch of ocean between Miami, Puerto Rico, and Bermuda.

It was on that journey that Alex had lost his hand and Stone had made a discovery that set the course of his future. While he did not yet understand everything he had discovered, he knew that special pyramids were scattered around the world, some in the most unlikely places, and that these pyramids were associated with sources of power. This pyramid, though a recent construction, was in the right general area, and was one of the few candidates he had not yet explored.

"I hope this isn't another dead end," Alex said. "On the positive side, at least you aren't forcing me to climb yet another mountain just because the peak looks triangular. What is it with you and climbing, anyway? Did you take up mountaineering after the service?" He often fished for information about what Stone had gotten up to after leaving the service.

"You can go back to your old job any time," Stone said with a grin.

"And leave you to your own devices? You wouldn't last a day without me."

"Keep telling yourself that," Stone said.

When they reached the pyramid, Stone's heart sank. He could tell immediately that there was no hidden doorway here. It was simply a monument that had been placed in an odd location. Not wanting to admit defeat, he made a circuit of the base, inspecting each stone.

Alex took off his rucksack and took out a brick-shaped contraption. He affixed a spiral antenna to the top and turned it on. It emitted a high-pitched squeal, which squelched into a low crackle as Alex fiddled with the dials. His ginger eyebrows shot up as he looked at the display.

"What is it?" Stone asked.

"I'm getting a powerful signal. This is a radiation hotspot." He held up the device, turned it around for Stone to see the angry red lights on the front. Alex was a brilliant inventor, and Stone had used a portion of his inheritance to hire him on. Some of the contraptions he and their friend Moses Gibbs built were truly remarkable.

"Maybe there's a piece of meteorite in here?" Stone asked, nudging a block with his booted toe.

Alex shook his head. "The signal is far too strong." He looked at Stone, eyes gleaming. "I think we're on to something."

"I don't understand how that contraption works, so I'll have to take your word for it," Stone said, his heart racing in anticipation. Alex was a brilliant engineer, mechanic, and man of science, and Stone had already come to rely on him in the short time he'd been home. If Alex said there was an odd phenomenon here, it was worth exploring.

"I don't suppose there's a door in that thing?" Alex inclined his head in the direction of the pyramid.

"No. If there's a way in, it must be underground. We'll have to look around."

Alex rolled his eyes. "More walking. If fun like this keeps coming I might blow my wig."

They began to search, walking in a circle around the pyramid, working their way outward. After ten minutes, Stone decided to change tactics.

"It doesn't take two of us to do this," he said. "You

keep going. I'm going to search around."

Alex smirked. "Don't let me catch you napping in the shade while I do all the work."

"Not a chance."

Stone's sharp eyes picked out a dense thicket heavy with young pine trees. It stood out bright green among the older, sturdier oaks. Inside it, he found a tiny graveyard. He immediately noticed that the rusted wrought iron fence was laid out in a pentagonal shape. Highly unusual. The gravestones were simple, hand-hewn, the names and dates so washed out that they were almost illegible. There were five of them, one set near each corner of the fence. Standing in the center was a badly eroded obelisk. At its base lay a large stone slab. Engraved on it were a sunburst and a cross. Above these symbols was the name JA Weishaupt along with the dates May 2, 1776-July 4,1776.

Stone frowned, took the sight in. There was more here than met the eye. And then he put it all together.

"Alex! Come here!" he shouted.

Alex hurried over. "What is it?" He glanced down at the large slab. "The kid only lived two months? And died on Independence Day? That's sad."

Stone shook his head. "This isn't a real grave."

Alex ran a hand through his ginger hair. "How can you be sure?"

"Take a close look at the sunburst. What do you see?"

Alex knelt for a closer look. He reached to touch a smaller image engraved at the center of the image. "The All-Seeing Eye is carved in the middle of the sun. It's so faint I didn't see it at first."

Stone nodded. "And what about the cross?"

"It's a double-barred cross," Alex said, a note of surprise in his voice.

"And look at the outline of the fence. It's pentagonal, but if you were to draw lines between the corners, it becomes..."

"A pentagram," Alex said thoughtfully. "But what does it all mean?"

"These are all symbols associated with a group founded by Johann Adam Weishaupt on May 2, 1776. It's a group many believed had among its members some of our Founding Fathers."

Alex sprang back from the false grave as if it were infectious. "The Illuminati! You think it's real?"

Stone grimaced. The question brought back memories of his past, things he had faced during his time in the service and in the intervening time before he had returned home the previous year.

"I believe so," Stone said. "Here. Help me move this slab."

"I'm not going to be of much help with one hand," Alex said. "Can't you move it yourself, mister football hero?"

"Stop trying to dodge the hard work, you laggard. You're plenty strong, and I don't want to accidentally break this."

Carefully, they worked the slab free and scooted it to the side. Beams of morning sunlight filtered through the canopy of forest above them cast the space beneath it in a golden glow. Beneath them lay an empty vault, six feet long, three wide, and four deep. The floor was lined with gray flagstone, and a symbol was etched in the center stone.

Alex sprang nimbly down into the vault and knelt over the symbol. "It's the square and the compass, the Freemasonry symbol. But it looks like it was scratched into the surface in a hurry. Like they wanted it known that they'd been here." He looked up at Stone and frowned. "Why would…"

He didn't get to finish the question. At that moment, the floor beneath him gave way and, with a shout of surprise, he fell from sight.

INTERLUDE 1

May, 1927
Five Years Ago

Brock Stone had been cold before, but this place was different. The wind sliced through his layers of clothing and numbed him to the bone. He moved robotically, his boots crunching through the frozen crust and plunging deep into the snow beneath. High above, a single cloud drifted across the azure sky like a ship adrift at sea. The sight filled him with sadness. It also strengthened his resolve.

He kept climbing, ascending the frozen slope with painstaking slowness. The stark white peak in the distance seemed to grow no closer. Not that he planned on going that far.

"Just a little bit farther." It was a refrain had repeated at least twenty times since beginning his ascent. The truth was, the few locals who had been willing to talk with him had provided only a general idea of where his destination lay, and not a single guide had been willing to take the job, even after he offered to triple their pay.

In the distance, he caught a glimpse of something moving. He squinted, shielded his eyes. Something was moving up the surface of a sheer cliff up ahead. It appeared to be human, or at least roughly shaped like one. Perhaps a Tibetan macaque? He immediately dismissed the idea. The altitude was far too high, and if he didn't miss his guess, the thing was closer to the size of a fully grown man. Perhaps that meant the monastery was close by!

"Hello!" he shouted. No response. "Can you help me?" The figure kept climbing.

With renewed vigor, Stone fought his way up the frozen slope, slipping and sliding but still moving upward until he finally reached the base of the cliff. Chest heaving from exertion, he took a few steps back and looked it up and down. The climber had vanished. Stone needed to hurry if he was to catch up.

"Would it have killed you to answer me?" he grumbled as he began his ascent. Stone had been climbing since his youth in Virginia, but this was one of the more challenging free climbs he had ever made. He picked out handholds and footholds that weren't slick with ice and slowly worked his way up.

Despite long years of experience, Stone found the going slow. His muscles were weary from hours of mountaineering and the climb itself was fraught with peril. The person he had seen climbing had moved much faster. Probably the locals had created their own path, like the cliff dwellers of the American Southwest. The latter had also incorporated false trails in the form of superfluous handholds that led the climber off the path, so that someone who did not know the correct path could find himself stuck hundreds of feet off the ground. Hopefully, that would not be the case here.

About twenty feet from the top of the cliff he paused to catch his breath. He looked out at the white mountains. One imposing peak stood about above the others. It had been known by many names over the years. The Chines had dubbed it Shèngmǔ Fēng, which roughly translated to 'Peak of the Goddess.' Tibetans called the peak

Chomolungma, or 'Mother of the Universe." In Sanskrit, it was Devgiri, meaning 'Holy Mountain.' But the English speaking world knew it as Mount Everest.

Named for British surveyor Sir George Everest, Everest was the tallest mountain in the world. None had yet reached its summit, though many had tried. But that mountain held no interest for Stone. He did not climb for glory.

It was only Stone's sharp hearing that saved his life. He heard a soft sound above him, like someone tiptoeing barefoot on a hard surface. He glanced up to see a boulder come tumbling over the edge of the cliff directly above him.

He swung to the side, hanging on with one hand as the boulder tumbled by, missing him by inches. His shoulder wrenched under the burden of his full body weight, but he held on. Desperately he searched for a foothold but his boots found none. His free hand found a crack in the frozen rock and he forced his fingers inside. It wasn't much of a grip, but it prevented him from plunging to his death.

All of his weight was now on his frozen fingers. His grip was slipping.

"Maybe this wasn't such a good idea after all," he grunted, struggling to hang on. Suddenly, all the unanswered questions seemed insignificant in the face of death. The toe of his right boot caught on something—the remnants of a woody plant that had once grown from the cliff face.

Now secure in his position, he looked around, his eyes scanning the cliff, searching for the path he had followed once before. A shadow appeared above him. He tensed, but no more boulders fell. Instead, a rope dropped down beside him.

Smiling, Stone took hold of the lifeline and began to climb.

3—THE LUMBER CAMP

Everyone looked up when Trinity Paige, clad in a khaki shirt, boots, and snug-fitting dungarees, strode into the middle of the camp. She saw confusion there, even curiosity, but little of the hunger one might expect from men who had been sequestered in a logging camp for Lord knew how long. Not that such looks would have stopped her. She had a job to do.

"That is one cutie patootie," a young man whispered to the man standing beside him. "I wish she was my filly."

"You have never ridden horse," the man replied in a thick, German accent.

"Filly means a pretty dame," the young man said, grinning.

"I know." The German's simple reply wiped the smile off the youth's face and elicited laughter from all the lumberjacks within earshot.

Suppressing a grin, Trinity chose her target, not the biggest man in the group, but the meanest looking. She marched right up to him, her eyes locked on his.

"Do you have a foreman around here?" she snapped.

"What do you think?"

"I think you don't know the answer to my question or else you'd have answered me." She punctuated the rejoinder with a sly smile.

It worked. The man's hard tone softened and there was a twinkle of amusement in his eye.

"You want Davis. He's the big fellow who's always sitting on his behind." The fellow flicked a glance off to his left.

"Bosses. You should see the backside on mine." She spread her hands a good three feet apart. It wasn't true, but it got her a few laughs. It was better to have people laughing with you than laughing at you.

Davis examined her the way a man might look at an unexpected blister on his privates. For her part, Trinity examined and assessed him in an instant: big, soft, slack-jawed, vacant stare. Probably got this job because he knew someone, not because he was a good lumberjack. That might be bad for the crew but a plus for her. She had a nose for things that didn't belong.

"I'm Trinity Paige, reporter for the *Washington Scribe*," she said. "I'm here to investigate reports of deaths."

Davis didn't rise from his seat on a stump. He took a sip of coffee, swished it around, and spat it on the ground.

"Nobody's died," he said. "Those are just rumors."

"How about Sam Price?" She posed the question loud enough for others to hear. You never knew who might be listening and what they might be able to tell you.

"He quit."

"Can you show me his letter of resignation?" She kept the questions coming at a rapid clip, trying to delay the moment when the man realized Trinity had no authority over him and kicked her out of his camp.

"We don't use those out here, city girl." Everyone laughed. "He walked off the job."

"Where could he have walked? There's no bus station

or railroad depot around here."

"Probably hitched a ride."

"He never returned home," Trinity said. "In fact, he hasn't been seen in weeks."

Davis shrugged. "Not my problem."

"How about Jarvis Lincoln?" she pressed.

"That one was an accident. Injuries happen on the job. It's not like getting your hair done. This is man's work."

"But you said there were no deaths."

"He was alive when they took him. Must have died afterward." His cheeks turned scarlet. He had let something slip that he had meant to keep secret.

"Who is *they* and where did they take him?" She had him on the ropes now.

"People from the lumber company. They took him to Seattle."

"John Kane's people?"

"I don't know any John Kane." The lie was evident in Davis' shifty eyes.

"He pays your salary," Trinity said.

Davis shrugged.

"What about the women who disappeared? Do you know anything about that?"

The young lumberjack who had commented on Trinity's looks spoke up. "That ain't us. It's the forest. It's cursed."

"Shut your mouth, Willy," Davis snapped. He finally stood and stepped forward so that he towered over Trinity. She didn't back down despite his rank body odor and coffee breath. "You listen to me, lady," Davis said. "I don't know a John Kane and there has been no string of deaths or disappearances. You tell your newspaper that.

Now, get out of here. We've got work to do."

Trinity was tempted to refuse, but if Davis wanted her gone she stood little chance of stopping them. And she was not about to give these great oafs an excuse to manhandle her.

"May I quote you on that?" she asked, by way of a parting shot.

"I don't care what you do. Just do it outside of my camp. For *safety* reasons." The smirk on Davis' face suggested he was not only talking about the possibility of an accident befalling her.

Trinity nodded, turned, and headed back the way she had come. It was a long way back to town, but at least she had rattled their cages. Despite what Davis said, men *had* gone missing from the camp. But what was happening to them?

She heard the rumble of an engine somewhere behind her, coming her way. Instinct told her to hide. Moving off the path and into the forest, she watched as Davis drove by in a battered truck. Trinity smiled. Unless she missed her guess, he was going to try to make contact with his superior. There was neither telephone nor telegraph in town, which meant he had a long drive ahead of him. If only she could be a fly on the wall when he finally made contact.

Her reporter's nose itching, she turned and headed back toward camp. Remaining hidden in the forest, she watched as the men finished their midday meal and returned to work. Among their ranks she spotted the young man Willy, who had spoken up earlier.

"There's my bird," she whispered. "Now to make him sing."

Keeping her distance, she followed until the two of

them were well clear of the others before making her presence known.

"Willy, may I speak with you?"

The young man nearly jumped out of his skin. "Jesus, Mary, and Joseph, lady! What are you doing here? If Davis catches you, he'll fire me and Lord knows what he'll do to you."

"Has he done things to women before?"

"That's not what I mean." Willy held up his hands. "He's got a temper, and there's no law out here to speak of. Everybody has to take care of their own selves."

"Believe me, I've dealt with far worse than Davis." Wasn't that the truth? If the young man only knew half of the things she had seen. "Besides, Davis just left."

Willy nodded. "Look, I don't want no trouble. I need this job."

"I'm not here to create any problems and I'm not looking for quotes for my article." At least, none with attribution, for the moment. "I'm going to be spending a lot of time in these woods and I need to know what to look out for."

Willy's blond locks flapped as he shook his head. "You shouldn't be out here at all. You're right. People have gone missing."

"Price?"

Willy nodded, then took a step back. "I don't want to talk about this."

"Please," she said. "I have a job to do and I won't leave until it's done. That I promise you. The question is, are you going to help me stay alive or not?"

His shoulders sagged and he closed his eyes. Trinity almost laughed. All men had the same body language when they finally gave in.

"Fine. A couple of us found Kennedy's body. He was all smashed up."

"Like a car crash?"

"Like he was pummeled to death with, I don't know, clubs, or rocks or something."

"What was done with his body?" She had to suppress the urge to take out a pad and start writing.

"We tried to tell Davis, but he wouldn't listen. He actually covered his ears. Said if anyone told him anything about it, they'd be fired on the spot. Anyhow, when we went back to bury him, his body was gone."

"Any idea what happened to him?"

"No. And I don't know anything else. We've had people go missing, the women in town have disappeared. If anybody in this camp knows what happened to them, they aren't talking." He looked around. "I really have to go."

"I understand. Is there anything else that might help me?"

Willy's dull expression suddenly turned sharp.

"Finish up this job of yours and get away from these parts as quick as you can."

4- THE CHAMBER

"Alex!" Stone jumped down into the crypt and knelt by the opening through which his friend had plunged. To his relief, Alex had fallen only a few feet. Now he sat gingerly rubbing his backside.

"Don't mind me," Alex said. "I'll just rest here for a while."

"Looks like you uncovered a trapdoor. Nice detective work." Stone climbed nimbly down into the vault and hauled Alex to his feet.

"I also found a hidden passageway." Alex pointed to a low tunnel that plunged down into the darkness.

"Excellent. Did you bring the flashlight?"

Alex shook his head in mock disapproval. "You would be utterly helpless without me." He dug into his pack and took out a silver cylinder. A crank was fitted into one end, and he turned it several times until the bulb on the other end flickered to life. He handed the flashlight to Stone. "After you, just in case the floor caves in again."

Stone barely managed to squeeze his broad shoulders through the narrow opening. He crawled along a low tunnel until the ceiling was high enough for him to stand. He cranked up the flashlight again and shone it ahead. The passageway sloped downward, heading in the direction of the pyramid, if he didn't miss his guess.

The air was cool and damp, and moisture trickled down the stone walls. Chill bumps rose on Stone's arms. Beside him, Alex shivered.

"I should have brought a jacket," Alex joked.

After a short walk, the two men found themselves standing before a heavy door. A brass knocker in the shape of the All-Seeing Eye hung there.

"If we knock do you think anyone will answer?" Alex asked.

"One way to find out." Feeling foolish, Stone grabbed the brass circle and rapped three times. The sound echoed through the stone passageway.

"Nobody home." Alex tried the big doorknob and confirmed that it was locked. "Not to worry." He once again dipped into his pack, took out a skeleton key, and began to work at the old-fashioned lock. "I was more adept when I had two hands. Not that it's anyone's fault." He cast a meaningful look at Stone.

"If I could buy you a new hand, I would," Stone said.

"Don't worry about it. For some reason, the ladies now find me fascinating. I haven't paid for my own drinks since our trip to the island."

"You've become such an optimist," Stone said. "A regular Pollyanna."

"I never read those books, but I saw the film." Alex grinned. "Mary Pickford?" He waggled his eyebrows.

"Are you going to pick that lock or shall I break the door down?" Stone said.

"Almost there." A few seconds later, Alex turned the knob and the door swung open.

Beyond the door lay an empty cave. Stone shone his light around. The beam climbed the walls up the to the apex of the high ceiling and back down to the bare floor.

"There's nothing here." Alex ran a hand through his hair. "Why the trapdoor and the hidden tunnel? Do you think this was a secret meeting place for the Illuminati?"

"Perhaps." Stone moved out into the chamber. He had spotted something unusual. Around the edges, the cave floor was smooth. In the middle, however, a square section about twelve feet across was rough, as if it had been broken up with hammer and chisel. He and Alex knelt for a closer look.

"It looks like something has been removed," Alex said, "but what?" And then his eyes brightened. "What if the pyramid up there…" He pointed at the ceiling. "Was originally down here?"

Stone shrugged. "I don't know. This chamber feels old… older than the pyramid in the field." He stood, looked around again. He felt as if they were missing something. And then his sharp eyes fell on a rough patch on the wall. Moving closer, he saw more chisel marks. "Look at this," he said to Alex.

Alex took the flashlight from Stone and inspected the spot carefully. He frowned, scratched his chin with the tip of his hook. "This looks like a coverup to me. Something was carved here. You can still see bits and pieces of the writing." He pointed at a patch the vandals had missed. There was a set of sharp, straight lines, smooth with age, that looked like writing. One complete figure looked familiar to Stone.

"This resembles the glyphs I discovered on the island in the Devil's Triangle." Stone shook his head slowly, considering this revelation. If this place were connected to the island, that meant it had something to do with his grandfather's work. It also meant that others, including John Kane, might be interested in finding it. That meant it was important.

"I assume whoever obscured the writing on the wall also removed whatever stood in the center of the cave," Alex said. "But what was here, and who took it?

"I don't know." Stone shook his head. "But I'm determined to find out."

5- CONSTANCE

Brock Stone stretched and breathed deeply of the evening air. Mist hung low over the Potomac River and the last traces of sunset painted the horizon pink. He was puzzled by what they had found in the hidden chamber. He had spent the afternoon in his grandfather's library, hoping to find the key to deciphering the mysterious glyphs. So far, he had found nothing helpful.

Stripping down to his skivvies, he waded into the cold water. He barely felt it, such was his mental focus. It was one of many skills he had acquired while studying with monks in Tibet. Isolated in his mental cocoon, he waded out until the water was waist-deep, then began to swim. He propelled himself against the Potomac's gentle current with powerful strokes. He was as committed to physical fitness as he was to mental acuity, and these regular swims were an important part of that discipline.

His sharp ears caught a low *thunk* in the distance, the sound of a wooden paddle striking a gunwale. He paused, treading water, and looked around.

About a hundred yards away, a young woman paddled a canoe. She was straining to maintain a straight course, whispering harsh curses every fourth or fifth stroke. As Stone watched, she steered the narrow craft toward the far shore, let out a stream of invective, and switched her paddle to the other side. She leaned into her strokes, digging the wooden blade deep into the water. The canoe began to tilt.

"Sit up straight," Stone called. "You're going to tip."

The warning did not have the desired effect. Instead, the woman let out a yelp and tried to stand. That was a mistake. The canoe capsized, dumping its occupant into the water.

Stone made a beeline for the woman, who broke the surface seconds later, sputtering and splashing. She went under, then came up again.

"Help!"

Stone reached her just as she went under again. He hooked an arm around her waist and lifted her out of the water. She struggled, kicking and flailing.

"Stay calm. I've got you." Stone kept his voice level. Far too often, drowning people managed to take their rescuers down with them.

"I can't breathe," the woman gasped.

"Yes, you can. I need you to lie back and let me support your weight. I will keep your head above water."

"Who are you?" she asked.

"My name is Brock Stone." He didn't know if his name meant anything to her. Why would it? But he felt her relax. As she floated on her back, he hauled her over to her canoe and she clung to it like a life preserver.

"Can you swim?" he asked. "Or at least keep your head above water until I can get you back to shore?"

She glared at him, intense blue eyes shining behind a curtain of sodden blonde hair. "Yes, I know how to swim, but my dress is weighing me down."

"Why would you wear a dress to go boating?" Stone laughed.

"Do you honestly think I haven't asked myself that question half a dozen times since I fell in?" She let out a sigh.

Stone nodded. "Think you can slip out of it?"

"You would like that, wouldn't you? Sorry, but I'm not some flapper."

Stone blinked. "Flapper? It's the 1930s."

The woman rolled her eyes. "Forgive me for having better things to worry about than what women of loose morals are called these days."

"Your moral superiority just might drag you down to the bottom of the river. Seriously, you will have a hard time keeping your head above water with it on. I promise won't look." He saw her hesitate and hurried on. "If it makes you feel any better, I'm in my shorts."

The woman rolled her eyes. "That makes it worse, actually. Oh, fine. Just stay close by and make sure I don't drown."

Holding on to the upturned canoe with one hand, she first removed her shoes one by one and handed them to Stone. Next, after a great deal of effort and a few more curses, she managed to free herself from her dress, which she flung at Stone. It struck him on the cheek with a cold, wet slap.

"I'll pull the canoe, you hang on to the stern. Feel free to push if you're able."

"I think I can manage."

"Good," he said, taking hold of the bow and beginning to swim. "By the way, do you have a name?"

"Constance Cray."

"A pleasure to meet you, present circumstances notwithstanding."

When they reached the shore Stone turned his back while Constance wrung out her sodden dress and slipped it back on. The damp fabric clung to her shapely figure, and Stone tried not to look. He was a gentleman, and he had a girlfriend who was prone to jealousy.

Once he, too, was dressed, he invited her up to his house. Stone was a private person, but it would not be chivalrous to put Constance back in her canoe and send her on her way.

"You can have a cup of tea, warm up and dry off. Then I will take you and your canoe to wherever you were headed."

"I would prefer black coffee," she said. "And this is my intended destination."

"What's that?" he asked.

"I came to see you."

Stone scratched his head. "And it didn't occur to you to use the front door?"

The corners of Constance's mouth twitched up. "I'm a friend of Trinity Paige. She tells me you have all sorts of advanced security measures set up around your property, especially along the drive."

Trinity Paige was Stone's girlfriend and a reporter at the *Washington Scribe*. She had a meddlesome nature that she passed off as a "reporter's nose." When not working on a story, Trinity passed her time criticizing her longtime love interest.

"She exaggerates," Stone said. "Besides, I also have security in place on the back side of the house." He frowned. It occurred to him that Trinity had never mentioned a friend named Constance.

"May I ask how you know Trinity?"

"I am a librarian. I sometimes help her with her investigative work." She looked around nervously. "It's the sort of thing my superiors at the library would frown upon."

"I promise you no one from the library is hiding among the trees." Stone smiled and his tension eased.

"And no one here will tell on you. I give you my word."

They made their way up the gentle, grassy slope to Riverbend, the Georgian Colonial mansion he'd inherited from his grandfather. Surrounded by dense forest, the three-story brick home was invisible to passersby, and its unobtrusive dirt driveway afforded little hint that so impressive a structure lay at its end. For that reason, Stone had few visitors, which was the way he preferred it.

The aroma of coffee and the steamy gurgle of the percolator greeted them as they stepped inside. Two men sat at the kitchen table reading the evening newspaper. One was Alex, the other was a muscular man with dark brown skin. Moses Gibbs was one of Stone's oldest friends. His grandfather had been caretaker of Riverbend. After a brief career in prizefighting, Moses had returned home to take up the post.

"Coffee's almost ready," Alex said. "I know you like a cup after your evening swims."

"Thank you. What's new in the news?"

"A woman named Amelia Earhart, a pilot, just made a trans-Atlantic flight from the US to Ireland. Better watch out, Stone. Trinity will want to go for her pilot's license soon."

Moses looked at Alex and grinned. "Just wait until Trinity finds out about the Flying Wing we're working on."

Stone cleared his throat. "Alex English, Moses Gibbs, may I introduce Constance Cray."

The two men hastily pushed back their chairs and stood.

Alex banged his knees on the table. "Sorry about that. I'm all arms and legs. And one hook, though I'm not a pirate captain." He held out his left arm.

Grinning, Constance grabbed the hook and gave it a firm shake. "Pleasure to meet you. Peter Pan is my favorite play. I saw it performed in London last year."

"Good to meet you, Ma'am." Moses gave a quick bob of his head.

Constance hesitated, her brow crinkling in a frown. People were often taken aback by Moses being treated as a member of the family rather than hired help. She forced a smile. "It is good to meet you, too." Her tone was sincere, but she did not offer to shake hands.

"If you all will excuse me, I've got some work to do." Moses gave another nod and left the kitchen.

"Don't you dare try it without me!" Alex called behind him.

"Try what out?" Stone asked. He glanced at Constance, whose face was marred by a puzzled frown. "Alex and Moses are inventors. I'm always looking forward to what they come up with next."

Alex waggled his hook at his friend. "It's a surprise. Oh, and I might have found a clue relating to our work this morning. I'll tell you about it later."

Alex filled three cups with steaming coffee and handed one to Constance and the other to Stone. In the short time since he had lost his left hand, he'd become surprisingly adept with the hook.

"Thank you," Constance said, accepting the cup. She took a sip and closed her eyes. "It's strong."

"I like it that way, "Alex said as he returned to his seat.

"As do I." Constance said.

She smiled a bit too beatifically, in Stone's estimation. He quirked an eyebrow but didn't comment. No sense messing things up for his friend.

"So, the two of you live together?" Constance asked.

"We do," Stone said. "My grandfather left me this place but it's far too big for only me, so I convinced Alex to move in. He's taken over most of the third floor."

"Not most. Only three rooms." Alex shrugged. "One for living, one for sleeping, and the third for tinkering." Alex was an engineer and a mechanical wiz. He was always hard at work on some new invention or an improvement on existing technology.

"Constance is a friend of Trinity's," Stone said. "May I call you Constance?"

"Of course you may."

"You are welcome to call me Brock, but I probably won't answer. Everyone calls me Stone."

"Because of the thickness of his head," Alex added.

Constance let out a tiny laugh, but her smile faded immediately.

"Trinity is the reason I'm here. I haven't heard from her in days and I'm worried. Have you spoken with her?"

Stone scratched his head, thinking. "It's been several days, but that's not unusual for Trinity. She told me not to worry. She's in New Jersey covering the investigation into the Lindbergh kidnapping. They found that little boy's body, you know. She said she might be keeping odd hours."

Constance flicked a glance at Stone, took a deep breath, and closed her eyes. "I made a promise to Trinity. If she went five days without calling me, I was to deliver a message to you."

Stone sat up straight, a chill running down his spine. "What message?"

Constance let out a sigh. "She put it in writing, and I fear the water ruined it." She took out a soggy envelope and handed it to Stone.

He took out the sheet of paper inside and unfolded it. As Constance had feared, the writing was smeared and illegible. He could only make out a few words:

Jefferson

Clark

John Kane.

"That's odd," Alex said, gazing intently at the paper. "That thing I discovered about the place we visited today." He hesitated.

"Go ahead. If it might be connected to whatever Trinity is investigating, I don't think we need to keep it a secret from Constance."

"After Jefferson took office, he began aggressively searching for sites associated with the Illuminati. He wrote in his journal about a map of the West found in an Illuminati temple that he described as 'nearly on his doorstep.'"

"Virginia, then," Stone said.

"Not long after that, the Lewis and Clark expedition headed West." Alex looked at Stone, shrugged. "The connection is thin."

Stone scratched his chin. "The search for the pyramids has been linked to John Kane from the start. But Lewis and Clark?" Stone looked at Constance. "I need you to tell me everything you know about what Trinity is up to."

6- THE PURSUIT

The *Flying Wing* that Alex and Moses had built was a modified version of the *Emsco B-8*, a two-seat, single-engine, low-wing, twin-boom experimental aircraft designed by Charles Rocheville in 1930. Unlike the original aeroplane, in which the pilots sat in tandem open cockpits, this aircraft featured an enclosed cockpit with four seats and a small cargo area, and boasted a broader wingspan and a larger fuel capacity. Rocheville had designed his craft for long-distance flight and had intended to fly it from Seattle to Tokyo. Fittingly, Seattle was their destination.

Constance knew that Trinity had traveled to the Pacific Northwest. She did not know what, exactly, Trinity was investigating but admitted she had made inquiries about Kane's business dealings on Trinity's behalf. The news was unsurprising to Stone, but still unwelcome. Kane was a dangerous man, but Trinity had a fearlessness that bordered on recklessness. Stone had long ago given up on trying to rein her in.

"You're sure this thing will get us there?" he said to Alex.

"We've made it to Montana and haven't had a problem yet," Alex said. He sat in the copilot's seat while Moses piloted the plane. "And if our new project works out as well as this one, Moses and I are going to be famous."

"When are the two of you going to stop keeping this big secret?" Stone asked. "After all, it's my money you're spending."

"Believe me, when this thing is ready, it's going to make us all rich."

"Stone's already rich," Moses said, his eyes locked on the sky in front of them.

"Really? Trinity didn't tell me that." Constance smiled at Stone. Stone had not wanted her to come along, but she had insisted that if they did not include her in the search for Trinity, she'd conduct her own search. Given the potential dangers involved in any investigation that touched on John Kane, Stone had felt it would be wrong to let her make a go of it alone. At least this way he could keep an eye on her.

"Speaking of Trinity, do we have any idea yet where to even look for her? Aside from somewhere in or around Seattle?" Alex asked.

Before Constance could reply, Moses spoke up. "There's a plane coming right at us."

Stone leaned forward and peered through the cockpit. Moses was right. A biplane was making a beeline for them. Stone recognized it right away. It was an *Albatross D.V.*, the World War I era German fighter plane that preceded the better known and much more reliable *Fokker D.VIII.*

"We're in the middle of nowhere," Alex said. "The odds of encountering another plane out here must be microscopic."

"Try changing course and see if it follows us," Stone suggested. He had a bad feeling about this newcomer.

Alex adjusted their course several degrees west-northwest. Moments later, the *Albatross* too changed its direction. Soon it was gaining ground on the *Flying Wing*.

"They's definitely after us," Moses said. If he was frightened, he didn't let it show. "Now I'm wishing we had added weapons to this bird."

"We designed her for long-distance travel," Alex said. "A weapons system would add unnecessary weight."

"It feels pretty necessary right now, don't it?" Moses said.

"Maybe they don't mean us any harm," Constance said. "Just another pilot out enjoying the day?"

The *Albatross* answered her question by opening fire. Bullets zipped past the nose of the *Flying Wing*. Alex let out a yelp and opened up the throttle.

"Can we outrun them?" Moses asked.

"Not likely," Stone said. "The *Albatross* was a lousy plane, but she's lighter, faster, and more maneuverable than we are."

"What do we do, then?" Alex asked, his face ashen and his voice tight.

"Head for that cloud bank up ahead. And don't fly in a straight line. A moving target is harder to hit."

"Roger that." Alex banked the plane toward starboard. Another rattle of gunfire and another hail of bullets missed them badly.

"And don't fall into a pattern with your movements," Stone warned. "Mix it up. Keep him guessing."

"How about you make me a list?" Alex snapped as he once again banked the plane to starboard, then back to port. "Sorry. This is my first dogfight."

"Don't mention it. But speaking of dogfights, I want to see if maybe we can turn this into a real battle. Can you lower the hatch?"

"Sure, but make sure you affix the safety line to your belt. I don't want you getting sucked out of the plane."

Stone did as instructed. Moments later a rumbling sound filled his ears and the deck trembled as a hatch opened beneath them. Wind ripped through the cabin like a tornado. Constance let out a shout of protest and covered her head. Stone grabbed hold of a metal rung at the edge of the hatch, drew his Webley Top-Break revolver. The standard-issue sidearm for the British army, it fired .455 slugs and delivered a punch. Stone worked his head and shoulders down through the opening.

The wind tore at him and he held on for dear life. Hanging upside down, he took a few seconds to reorient himself before taking aim at the *Albatross* as it closed in. The pilot fired off another burst, but at this range and with his poor accuracy, he was wasting ammunition. An amateur.

Stone took aim with his Webley, and focused. He squeezed off a single shot aimed at the cockpit. It missed, making a ragged tear in the upper wing. Stone fired again and this time the slug pinged off the fuselage just inches from the cockpit.

The pilot took evasive action, sending the fighter into a barrel roll, then taking it into a dive, before coming up and firing again. Stone adjusted his angle and squeezed the trigger. This time his shot struck the landing gear.

"I can't get a decent shot," he complained, though no one could hear him. As the battle went on, the Albatross drew ever closer. Stone managed to score a few hits, one to the cockpit's windscreen, which slowed the pursuit a little, but nothing that made the Albatross back off. Finally, when he had emptied the cylinder, he climbed back into the cabin.

"No joy," he said. "I hit them a few times but it's like poking an elephant with a sharp stick."

"We're almost into the cloud bank," Alex said. "But what do we do after that?"

"We got parachutes," Moses offered.

Constance blanched. "I don't know how to use one of those things."

"Forget it," Stone said. "We'd be sitting ducks. The pilot would gun us all down before we hit the ground." He looked around. "Are you sure there aren't any weapons on board?"

Moses looked at Alex. "I suppose we could show him the new invention."

Alex shook his head. "It's not a weapon. Besides, he hasn't even had a chance to test it out yet."

"But if he…"

"There's no time to argue," Stone said. "Tell me about this new toy of yours."

INTERLUDE 2

May, 1927
Five Years Ago

Stone grabbed hold of the rope and tested its strength before grabbing on with both hands. It supported his weight. He looked up, trying to catch sight of his rescuer. A small, wiry man with skin like tanned hide, peered over the ledge.

"I will not pull you up," the man said simply.

"Fair enough." With the rope to hold on to, Stone had no problem finishing the climb. When he reached the top, he found himself on a narrow path that wound its way along the mountainside.

The man who had come to his aid neither spoke to him nor met his eye. Stone was six feet three inches tall. This fellow barely came up to his shoulder. He was dressed in layers of worn clothing and wore a knife with a bone hilt in a leather sheath at his hip. Silently, the man knelt and gathered his rope.

"Thank you for your help," Stone said.

"You are welcome." Still no eye contact.

"My name is Brock Stone."

The man continued coiling his rope without acknowledging that Stone had spoken.

"Was it you I saw moving along the ridge a few minutes ago?"

"No." The fellow stood and secured his rope to his belt. Stone had met a few silent types in his time, but this man took it to the extreme.

"I'm looking for something. Perhaps you could help me."

"Shambhala." The little man sneered. "Many other fools die searching for a legend. You should turn back."

So, the fellow could string two sentences together when he felt like it. "I am not looking for Shambala. I seek Kanchinjínga."

If the fellow recognized the name, he didn't show it. His expression remained impassive. "If you are a treasure hunter, you will be disappointed." The name Kanchinjínga meant "the five treasures of the high snow."

"I know about the monastery." Stone didn't miss the way the man's left eye twitched at the mention of the name. "Did you come from there?"

"No."

"So, there *is* a monastery on this mountain!" Stone was relieved.

"That was not the question you asked." With that cryptic reply, the man turned and strode away.

"Can you show me where it is?" Stone called. When the fellow didn't reply, he followed along behind him. "Mister, I'm sorry to interrupt your busy day, but I have come a very long way."

"And you have a very long way yet to go," the man said without looking back.

"I assume you mean that metaphorically," Stone sighed. "Do you at least have a name?"

"I do."

"Are pedantic replies what passes for wisdom at the monastery, or is it only you who takes pride in such pettiness?"

The little man flashed a sly grin over his shoulder.

"You are not a complete fool, then."

"Perhaps not complete," Stone said, still following along. "But I did travel all this way without actually knowing how to find the monastery."

"That was foolish, indeed." There was a note of amusement in the fellow's voice that set Stone's teeth on edge. "You may not know my true name, but other white men call me Gideon. Do not bother telling me what you are called."

"All right, Gideon. Will you please show me the way to the monastery? I can pay you."

"What makes you believe there is a monastery here?" Gideon asked, quickening his pace.

Stone scrambled to keep up. He was a skilled climber and kept himself in tip-top physical condition, but despite his longer stride, he found himself losing ground on Gideon with every step. It was time to play the only card he held.

"I walked the Path of the Five Pecks of Rice," Stone called. His heart pounded. He wondered how great a risk he was taking by admitting this. His grandfather always told him, *You can never go wrong with the truth.* He had a feeling he was about to put that theory to the test in a way Granddad had never anticipated.

Gideon froze, slowly turned to face Stone. "If that is true, then you gave up the fairer sex for nothing. Those men were fools who spouted nonsense."

"That's not what I'm talking about, and you know it," Stone took a step forward. "I can see it in your eyes." He held his breath, waited.

Gideon's eyes bulged and he strode back along the trail in Stone's direction. "You see nothing!" Finally, the man showed some emotion, even if it did appear to be anger.

"I found the pyramid" Stone went on. "I saw what was underneath."

"You should stop speaking," Gideon said. Despite the rage burning in his eyes, his demeanor was once again calm, his voice placid.

Stone was beyond worrying about what Gideon might try to do to him. He was desperate.

"I have stood before the Celestial Master."

Gideon halted inches from Stone. "I do not know where you learned those words, but you should not have spoken them aloud. Because you are an ignorant child, I will forgive you once." He held up a finger. "Now leave this place and never come back. He pivoted on his heel and took a step.

"Gideon, wait." Stone reached out to seize the man's arm.

As if he had eyes in the back of his head, Gideon whirled around just before Stone's fingers touched him. With a lightning-fast motion, he struck Stone's forearm at a spot just above the wrist. Stone's arm immediately fell limp.

Though taken by surprise, Stone was a seasoned fighter and blessed with exceptional strength and speed. Instinctively he moved out of the way as Gideon's roundhouse kick whizzed past his head, so close that it brushed Stone's chin whiskers. In the narrow confines of the mountain trail, he was not able to avoid Gideon's next strike—a spinning side kick that sat the larger man down on his backside."

Stone felt like the overbearing drunk who had just been streeted from the speakeasy. For a split second, his fingers itched for his sidearm. It was instinctive, a response to danger that had been drilled into him. The impulse made him sad. He no longer wanted to be that man. But he didn't know how to be anything else.

"How did you know I was about to touch you?" Stone asked.

"I use more than my eyes."

"Did you learn that at the monastery?" Stone hoped to catch the man off guard with the question, get him to betray something. Gideon's response surprised him.

"That and many other things." The little man's eyes twinkled with mischief. "You asked if I came from the monastery. At the moment, I am returning there."

"Is everyone there so literal?" Stone asked, climbing to his feet and brushing himself off.

"When it suits our purposes." Gideon folded his arms and looked Stone up and down. "Why do you seek the Five Treasures?"

Stone searched for words adequate to describe the changes wrought in him over the past four years. The shattering of his illusions, the breaking of his very foundations.

"I need something to believe in again," he said.

The two men stared at one another in silence. Deep down, Stone felt as if his entire future hinged upon this moment.

Finally, Gideon gave a small shake of his head. "I will not show you the way, Brock Stone." Stone's heart sank. "But I will not stop you from trying to follow me."

With that, the little man turned and began climbing up the steep cliff.

Stone blinked twice, then followed. He had only climbed about ten feet when the full meaning of Gideon's words hit him.

"I never told him my name."

7- STALKED

This was all Brock Stone's fault. He was the one who had set Trinity on John Kane's trail. If it weren't for him, she would never have come to this wilderness in the first place. She was tired, dirty, and hungry, but she could live with those things. What she could not abide was failure.

"If that old man lied to me, I will give him a piece of my mind, and the toe of my boot in his…" A shiver ran through her, cutting her off in midsentence. Between the deep shadows and the altitude, she never felt warm in this forest. Goosebumps rose on her flesh and she rubbed her hands together for a little warmth.

"How much longer should I search before I give up?" she wondered aloud. Anger made her cheeks burn. She had swallowed the old prospector's story hook, line, and sinker. He had seemed so earnest. "He must have a background in theatre," she mumbled. Then again, she had only given the small slot canyon a cursory search before moving on to the larger box canyon, which she had mostly inspected from the cliffs above. There remained a great deal of ground to cover if she intended to make a thorough search.

She shrugged off her backpack and took out a map. She sat down on a log, unfolded it, and searched for her location. She laughed when she found it. A dot labeled Rockmire amidst a sea of green.

"You bought a map without even looking at it to see if it would be of use." Cursing, she crumpled it into a ball and stuck it into her backpack. It would make good tinder should she need to start a fire.

She glanced up at the sky, scarcely visible among the treetops that lined the narrow canyon. Faint streaks of orange told her it was getting late. The sight turned her mood dark. She might not be able to make it out before dark. The thought sent a shiver down her spine. She wasn't afraid, exactly, but she didn't love the idea of camping out here, just in case the stories were true.

The path leading up to the slot canyon was hard to find and even harder to ascend. By the time she reached the top, she was soaked with sweat and her muscles felt like water. What a sight she must be. Not that there was anyone around to see her.

No sooner had the thought occurred to her than she had the sensation of being watched. She sprang to her feet and looked around. Noting but green. And then she heard a sharp crack, like a tree limb snapping. In the quiet it sounded like a gunshot. Someone was out here.

She stood there, tension tying her stomach into knots, waiting. Her heart thrummed, her breathing was loud and heavy. Except that wasn't the sound of her breath. It was someone else…or something else. The sound was a deep, wet, animal snuffling. And it was coming closer.

She considered her options. Should she try to run? Where could she go? Did the thing even know she was here? Perhaps the dense thicket of fir trees covered her scent. Maybe if she could just be quiet, it would go away.

She held her breath, sat motionless, and waited. The noise continued, circling the spot where she sat. And then a pungent odor, feral, almost sulfurous, washed over her, borne on the night air. She retched, her empty stomach flip-flopping.

My word, what is that?

But she knew what it was. She had gathered enough stories to be something of an expert. Dizzy with disbelief, she shrugged off her backpack and dug inside, searching for her camera. She should have had it at the ready, but the skeptic in her had quashed the idea.

And then the foul stench was gone. All was silent.

Trinity stood there, arm buried in her backpack, eyes searching the surrounding. Nothing moved. There was no sound but her ragged breathing. She took a few moments to let her heart rate return to something approaching normal.

"Foolishness," she scolded herself. "A wild animal passed somewhere close by and your imagination turned it into something else."

Just then, the foliage in front of her parted.

Trinity screamed.

8- THE DOGFIGHT

"What do you call this thing again?" Stone looked down at the strange suit he now wore. It was a set of coveralls made from a thin fabric that Alex assured him was exceptionally strong. Beneath each arm was a winglike membrane of the same fabric.

"I call it a soaring suit," Alex said from the pilot's seat. "Moses doesn't like the name."

"Neither do I," Stone said. "How do we know it will support my weight?"

"The suit we've tried out," Alex said. "Moses has flown in it and he weighs almost as much as you."

"It was almost like really being able to fly," Moses said. "Better than any parachute, that's for sure."

"It's the boots that haven't been flight tested," Alex continued. "But we fired them up in the lab and they didn't explode."

"That's comforting." Stone cast a nervous glance at the heavy boots he wore. They were high, with thick soles. A tube ran from the back of each up to the canister he wore on his back. In his right hand he held a cylinder with a button on the end that would activate the boots.

"I recommend firing the burners in short bursts to conserve fuel," Alex said. "You should have enough for about five minutes."

"What happens when I run out?"

"You sail on down to the ground," Moses said. "Just make sure you deal with that biplane before you do. Otherwise, it's gonna be open season."

"Thanks for that," Stone said.

"Speaking of the biplane, we're almost out of the clouds," Alex said. "If you want the element of surprise, you'd better get a move on."

"This had better work."

"Relax," Alex said. "I designed it, so you know it'll run smoothly."

"Like eggs in coffee," Moses added.

"This is remarkable," Constance said. "Like something out of Jules Verne."

"It's not that advance," Alex said, his cheeks turning pink. "It's based on work being done by several European inventors and scientists."

"Alex figures out the science. I just help him make it run," Moses said.

"You are both far too humble," Constance said. "I am amazed at what you have done with the plane, the suit, and whatever you call these things."

"Rocketboots," Moses said.

Constance nodded and turned to Stone. "Be careful."

Stone pulled on his goggles and grinned. "I don't think that's possible, considering what I'm about to do. But I'll give it my best shot."

Alex opened the hatch again and Stone climbed down the few rungs, holding on with all his might. The icy wind bit through him, and the cold moisture made it difficult to hold on. He was surrounded by impenetrable white mist.

Stone concentrated on his sharp sense of hearing. He mentally separated the rush of the wind from the roar of the *Flying Wing's* engines. Then he picked out the higher-pitched drone of the *Albatross*. He focused on the sound until he was certain of its location. He locked in on the spot and opened his eyes.

The sky was brighter, the air growing warmer. They were leaving cloud cover. Stone tensed to spring. They broke out into open sky. Stone focused on the cloud bank until he saw the fighter plane's silhouette appear.

And then he jumped.

He fanned his arms out and felt a sudden upward thrust as air filled the wings of the soaring suit. He really disliked that name. The biplane was emerging from the clouds and Stone angled toward it.

The pilot didn't see him coming until Stone was nearly on top of him. Instinctively he opened fire. Stone gritted his teeth expecting a sharp burst of pain and certain death. But the pilot had no time to change his course and the rounds came nowhere close to the man in the flying suit. Unfortunately, Stone had aimed too high and he shot past the biplane. The pilot looked up as Stone passed him by.

Cursing, Stone adjusted the suit and began a long, slow turn. As he came about, he looked up to see that the biplane had maintained its course and was closing in on the *Flying Wing*. Alex was taking evasive action, but the transport lacked the speed and agility of the smaller plane. It was all up to Stone.

He completed his turn and locked in on the fighter. His heart skipped a beat as his thumb found the button that would ignite his rocketboots.

"Alex, I hate being your guinea pig," he shouted. His voice was lost in the wind. Heart in his throat, he locked his legs as Moses had instructed him, and fired the burners.

A jolt of white-hot pain shot from his hips up his spine as he was hurled forward at high speed. In his ears, the scream of the wind rushing past him dueled with the sonic scream of the rocketboots. He felt his lips pushed back by the force of the air, baring his teeth in a rictus of adrenaline.

He released the button and adjusted his course so that he was following directly behind the fighter plane. Another burst of the rockets and in seconds he had closed half the distance between them. Still locked in on its target, the *Albatross* banked to the left as the gap between it and its quarry narrowed perilously. The pilot fired again and the rounds just missed the transport's tail section. Distress twisted Stone's gut. For a moment, he had been certain his friends were goners. It was time for an act of desperation.

Like a quarterback leading his receiver, Stone chose a path that would intersect with the banking aircraft, and hit the gas. He was hurtled forward like a bullet, so fast that the biplane seemed to be standing still. For a split-second Stone feared that he would overshoot his target. The pilot finally noticed him and let out a cry of alarm.

Everything seemed to happen in an instant. Stone released the gas. The pilot took his craft into a dive. Stone, inexperienced with the soaring suit, pressed his arms to his sides. He immediately began losing altitude. Too much altitude.

He soared beneath the fleeing biplane and slammed into its undercarriage. His breath left him, replaced by a flood of pain. The impact sent the plane into a barrel roll. Stone reached out in desperation and managed to hook his arms around the landing gear. The world somersaulted before him and he closed his eyes against the dizzying sight.

The engine whined and sputtered. The pilot spewed a stream of invective. Stone wondered if they would crash. And then he barked a laugh. The *Albatross* might crash, but thanks to the sailing suit, he didn't have to go down with it. But no sooner had the thought come to him than the pilot brought the craft out of the roll and righted his course.

"Now what?" Stone said to himself. He was unarmed and clinging to the landing gear. He could do no good from here.

The pilot once again drew a bead on the *Flying Wing*. Stone's collision with the biplane had gained the fleeing transport a few precious seconds, but not nearly enough. The fighter plane opened fire. From his position beneath the craft, Stone saw the rain of bullets seem to bend toward their target. A few more seconds and they would shred the transport plane to ribbons. Having no better idea, Stone flipped upside down and pressed the soles of his boots firmly against the plane at a spot he estimated to be underneath the pilot's seat.

"This had better work."

He activated the rockets. The impact nearly tore his shoulders from their sockets, but he held on to the landing gear with all his might. The average man would not have been able to maintain his grip, but Stone was not an average man. He held on with muscles that had been honed by years of strenuous training and enhanced in ways he didn't like to think about. Pain burned through even as the rockets burned through the thin aluminum hull.

It was only seconds, but it felt like hours before the

pilot let out a shriek of pure pain and terror. Stone released his grip on the landing gear and let himself fly free. As he sailed away, he glanced back to see the burning fighter plane tumbling toward the ground, leaving a trail of smoke behind him.

The pilot bailed out. He tumbled toward the ground, then activated his chute far too early. He hung there far above the ground as the strong wind began to carry him toward the distant mountains.

This was an opportunity Stone could not pass up. He turned and sailed toward the drifting pilot, who didn't see him coming. Stone wrapped his arms around the man as they collided, pinning his arms to his sides. Immediately they began to fall, the parachute unable to support his weight.

"What are you doing? You're going to kill us." His words cut off in a gurgle as Stone wrapped a powerful hand around his neck.

"Listen carefully. You answer all my questions or I'll cut your ropes and let you fall. Understand?" Stone didn't have a knife on him, but the pilot didn't know that. He nodded and Stone lessened his grip.

"Why did you attack our plane?"

"Orders," the man grunted. "You're being tracked. Pilots all over are on the lookout for you. If one of us spotted you, we were to report your location, then shoot you down, preferably somewhere witnesses wouldn't see."

"Who did your orders come from?"

"I don't know."

Stone once again tightened his grip on the man's throat.

"He's called the Warden."

Stone frowned. "And who do his orders come from?"

"I can't say for certain. He might have Senior Wardens above him. I wouldn't know. Ultimately, we all take our orders from the Worshipful Master. And don't bother asking his name. The only rumor I've ever heard about him is he's a rich guy from back East. That's all I know. I swear it."

"Are you Freemasons?" Stone asked.

Even in this perilous situation, the pilot let out a braying laugh. "The Freemasons are children playing at a game they don't understand."

"Who are you, then?"

Without warning, the pilot threw his head backward. Pain burst across the bridge of Stone's nose as skull collided with cartilage.

"That wasn't very nice," Stone said, blinking away the pain. Unlike himself, the pilot wore a knife at his belt. Stone pulled it free and began sawing at the parachute cords. The man screamed and fought, but Stone was too strong for him. "Don't feel bad. I don't know about you, but the gall is my favorite time of the year."

He severed the last cord and released the pilot. As the man plummeted toward the ground, Stone spread his arms and let the sailsuit arrest his fall. Spotting the *Flying Wing*, he set his course, braced himself, and fired the rocketboots. As he soared through the air, he had to smile.

"Alex my friend, I will never doubt you again."

9- THE NEWSPAPER

Seattle was not what Stone had expected. He had envisioned a small coastal town, an oasis on the outskirts of the dense forests of the Pacific Northwest. While the oasis analogy might have been apt, it was a far cry from a small town. Though it was no match for the bustling cities of the east, it was most definitely a city.

Alex had been grumpy since their encounter with the fighter. Although his rocketboots had worked remarkably well, they had burned out just as Stone returned to the *Flying Wing*. As they walked down the streets, his mood brightened and he excitedly pointed out prominent landmarks. Though he had never visited the west coast, he had studied up on their destination.

"That's Smith Tower," he said, pointing his hook in the direction of a skyscraper that dominated the skyline. It was topped by a pyramidal spire that shone in the sun. "It stands 484 feet tall. At thirty-eight stories it is the tallest skyscraper in the city."

"I can see that," Stone said.

"I would not want to be one of the men who helped build that thing," Moses said. "If I'm going to be that high in the air, I want wings and rocketboots."

"It's one of the tallest skyscrapers outside of New York City," Alex said, diverting the subject away from the rocketboots. "It's the tallest building west of the Mississippi."

"Actually," Constance said, "it's now the second-tallest. The Kansas City Power and Light Building overtook it just last year."

"Interesting," Alex said. He'd taken a shine to Constance and she seemed to share his interest, though they'd kept their interactions fully above board. "I hope we'll get to see the Aurora Bridge. It just opened in February and it's supposed to be a magnificent representation of cantilever and truss construction."

"It's also a favorite of suicide jumpers," Constance said. "Mostly broken-hearted lovers from what I hear."

"I can't imagine anyone would ever be so foolish as to break your heart," Alex teased.

"The newspaper office is just around the corner," Stone said loudly, cutting off their cloying banter before it could truly get underway. "You did say Trinity planned on visiting here?" he said to Constance.

"She specifically mentioned it during our last phone call."

Moses excused himself and crossed the street over to a city park where a group of men, working-class judging by their clothing, were gambling with dice. They were mostly white, but a few black and Chinese men were among their number and they invited Moses to join them. Stone smiled ruefully.

The office of the *Seattle Spokesman* was small, neat, and smelled strongly of ink. A young man in a cheap suit greeted them politely and asked their business.

"Brock Stone to see Mister Griffith."

"I am Mister Blinn. May I help you?"

"No." Stone didn't intend to be rude. He simply saw

no point in wasting time. "It is Mister Griffith we need to see."

"Do you have an appointment?"

"Mister Blinn," Constance said gently, nudging her way in front of Stone, "our friend and your colleague in the newspaper industry, Trinity Paige, is missing. We know she had a recent meeting scheduled with Mister Griffith. Did you, by any chance, meet her?"

Blinn's demeanor suddenly changed. "I remember her. Quite a tomato, that one." He grinned and waggled his eyebrows, but froze under Stone's cold glare. "I'll take you to Mister Griffith right away." He turned and led them through a bright green door into a smoke-filled office.

"There are people here to see you," Blinn said to the surprised-looking man seated inside.

Griffith was a stocky, bald man with a few strands of hair clinging stubbornly to the top of his shiny pate. He fingered his walrus mustache and stared at them over the top of a tiny pair of reading glasses.

"I wasn't expecting anyone," he rumbled.

"Brock Stone. It's a pleasure to meet you, sir." Stone stepped forward and gave him a firm handshake. "I appreciate you seeing us on short notice."

"But I didn't…"

"We are here about Trinity Paige," Stone continued, not permitting the man to finish his sentence. "She's missing and we understand you were the last person to see her alive."

"Now see here." Griffith rose from his seat, an unimpressive sight considering the top of his head came up to Stone's chin. His tone and demeanor suggested he was accustomed to bullying and browbeating his underlings, but he faltered under Stone's gaze. "I did meet with the woman," he continued, softer this time. "But that's all."

"Why did you meet with her?" Stone kept his tone firm but polite.

"Because she showed up unannounced and barged her way in here, just like you did. I warned young Blinn here," he nodded at his employee, whose face had turned a fine shade of pale, "not to let something like that happen again."

"It's my fault, I'm afraid." Constance moved up to stand beside Stone. "I'm terribly worried about Trinity and Mister Blinn was so kind to me."

Griffith's face softened as his eyes fell on Constance. "I'm sure he was." His tone was lascivious. Stone glared at him and the newspaper man's face turned scarlet.

"What can you tell us about the work Trinity is doing out here?"

"She's investigating an east coast businessman named Kane. I couldn't tell her much, just rumors."

"Any idea where she went?" Stone pressed.

"Kane has been conducting business in this area for about a decade. One area that has raised suspicion is his logging business."

"Why would that be suspicious?" Stone asked.

"It's not so much the business, but the rumors that surround it."

"What sort of rumors?" Constance said.

"Most of them are absurd, not even worth mentioning. One persistent rumor is that the company is covering up deaths inside their camp. Injuries and even deaths aren't uncommon in logging, but the men who do that kind of work all know the risks. Rumor has it the company is burying the bodies and claiming the men just walked off the job."

Stone wasn't sure what to make of this. "Mister Griffith, in your opinion, is this something worth investigating?"

Griffith shrugged. "I doubt it. Miss Paige seemed to lose interest in that topic fairly quickly. After that, she started asking ridiculous questions."

"That doesn't sound like Trinity," Constance said.

"What sorts of questions?" Stone asked.

"About monsters and ghosts. Nonsense and absurdities. I finally had to show her the door. Politely, of course."

"And you have no idea where she went when she left here?"

"None." Griffith forced a tight-lipped smile. "Now, if you will excuse me, I am a very busy man."

They thanked him for his time and left the office. On their way out, Blinn accosted them.

"I couldn't help but overhear part of your conversation." His cheeks turned scarlet under Constance's disappointed frown. "All of it, actually. The walls are thin." He cast a nervous glance in the direction of Griffith's door and lowered his voice. "Mister Griffith lied to you. Miss Paige did tell him what her next stop would be."

"More thin walls, I take it?" Constance said.

"Never mind that," Stone said. "Where was Trinity going next?"

Blinn grimaced. "It's a strange place. Some even say it is haunted."

10- THE SCHOOL FOR INSANE GIRLS

It was a beautiful day on Mercer Island. The sun sparkled on the waters of Lake Washington as Alex brought the rented Ford Model A Roaster pickup to a halt in front of a long, curving driveway that led to an imposing, three-story brick building.

"There it is!" Alex proclaimed. "The Martha Washington School for Insane Girls."

"That was never its name," Constance said. "And it is no longer a girls' home. It recently became a home and care center for babies."

"That Blinn fellow from the newspaper said it's haunted," Alex said.

Moses shuddered and made the sign of the cross. The big man wasn't afraid of much, but the subject of ghosts made him especially twitchy.

"They said the teachers were cruel to the students, violent even," Alex said, his voice suddenly husky, "and the students retaliated in kind. There were murders, suicides, and some even say occult rituals were performed here."

"I doubt that's what Trinity was here to investigate," Stone said before Alex launched into one of his lectures. "Constance and I will inquire inside. The two of you can wait for us."

"Fine by us. At least we didn't have to dress like we're going to church," Alex said.

Stone had traded his preferred khakis for a light brown summer suit with a six-button vest and a silk tie that had belonged to his grandfather. Constance was clad in a simple navy dress with wide shoulders and a belted waistline. She was all business.

They were greeted at the door by an officious-looking man in an ill-fitted black suit. He looked them up and down, frowning.

"Mister Stone, and Miss… something, I take it?"

Stone forced a smile. "I am Brock Stone and this is Constance Cray. We have an appointment with Mrs. Carroll."

"I am Mister Ward." Ward tilted his round, balding head, and peered between them. "Why did your driver not drop you off at the front door?"

"Our truck was leaking oil and we didn't want it fouling your driveway," Stone invented. "He has gone to make repairs." The truth was, they didn't know if the presence of Moses would create a problem.

Stone had been around the world and tolerant people were getting harder to find. In Germany, a fascist named Adolf Hitler was running for president. Remarkably, Hitler had led a failed coup against the government almost a decade earlier, and had served time in prison, yet he had now enjoyed tremendous popular support. It was like Stone's grandfather used to say, "Never underestimate the power of telling disillusioned people exactly what they want to hear." Other European nations were also facing similar right-wing uprisings. Upon returning home, the fuzzy memories of Stone's youth gave way to the reality that the nation he loved was battling the same forces of fear, mistrust, and intolerance that seemed to be driving Europe toward a second Great War.

Ward looked at him doubtfully, but finally nodded. "Please wipe your feet before you enter." He led them to the director's office.

Patricia Carroll was a tall, gangly woman with a large nose and short, gray hair. She welcomed them with a curt not and did not invite them to sit down.

"I am afraid I cannot tell you anything more than what I told your colleague, Miss Paige," she said.

"I'm afraid there has been a misunderstanding," Constance said. "Miss Paige is our friend. She has gone missing."

Carroll glared sharply at Ward, who was lingering in the doorway. "That was not the message you conveyed to me, Mister Ward."

Sweat broke out on Ward's brow. He ran a hand through his thinning black hair. "It was Junina who took the message, Headmistress. She has been having a difficult time of late. Ever since…"

"You may go!" Carroll said sharply. She narrowed her eyes slightly, as if trying to send a message to Ward.

Ward gave a bob of his head, turned, and hurried away. His heels clicked loudly on the marble floor as he fled. When the sound faded into silence, Carroll relaxed and motioned for Constance to close the door.

"I apologize. Junina was a resident here when this was a home for troubled young women. She does not have a place in the outside world, but she is quite bright, so I kept her on as a staff member."

"If I may, what do you mean she doesn't have a place?" Stone asked.

"She is a Yakama Indian by birth. No one around here will hire or marry her, and she refuses to return home. Something about a childhood trauma." Carroll gave a small, sad shake of the head.

"I am sure you are very busy, so we shall not demand much of your time," Constance said. "We are tracing our friend's last known movements. Might you have any idea where she went after she left here?"

Carroll shook her head. "We spoke only briefly. She was reporting on the history of this building, and I have only been employed here for a year. I told her what I knew, and then turned her over to Junina. No one knows this place the way she does."

"Do you know what they talked about?" Stone asked.

Carroll stiffened. "Of course not. I am not Mister Ward, lingering in doorways or hiding around corners."

"Please accept my apologies. I only wondered if Junina might have discussed their conversation with you."

Carroll closed her eyes for a moment and her shoulders sank. When she opened her eyes again, her demeanor had changed. "It is I who owe you an apology. Things have been difficult here. My staff believe the ridiculous ghost stories about this building, and I just learned that Ward has been encouraging them. He has them all convinced that a devil is buried beneath the old wine cellar. None of them will go near the place now. Of course, there is nothing down there but dusty old crates. It hasn't been used for wine storage since the original headmaster of the girls' home died."

"We understand," Constance assured her. "Would it be possible for us to speak with Junina?"

Carroll looked at them each in turn, as if taking their measure. Finally, she made a curt nod. "You may. She is working in the office near the front doors. I only ask that you stop questioning her if she becomes upset. She is fragile."

As they made their way to the office, they passed Ward. He was engaged in a quiet but intense conversation with a bear of a man clad in a dark green boilersuit. His arms and legs were like tree trunks, and he had no visible neck. Auburn hair was thin on his head, but thick on his neck, arms, and chest. He had a broad face, flat nose, and sharp, beady eyes that flashed with cunning. The man made a show of looking Constance up and down, and when Stone took a step toward him, he smirked and cracked his knuckles.

"Enough of that, Klaus," Ward snapped at the man. "You have work to do."

"Ja. Is true." Klaus locked eyes with Stone for a split second before vanishing down a flight of stairs. Ward offered a halfhearted apology and scurried away.

Stone shook his head. He had half a mind to speak to Klaus in private, but reminded himself that they had more pressing matters to attend to. They paused outside the office door.

"Listen," Stone began. "It won't take two of us to speak with Junina. You can handle that by yourself."

Constance frowned. "You aren't going after that ape of a man, are you? Because I don't need a white knight."

Stone grinned. Trinity had said much the same to him more times than he could count. "I'm going to look for the wine cellar she mentioned."

Constance frowned. "For what reason?"

"Just a hunch. It might be nothing, but if Ward doesn't want the staff poking around down there, maybe there's a secret he's hiding."

"What might that have to do with Trinity?"

"Probably nothing," Stone admitted. "But I sense Ward is hiding something, and Trinity has a much sharper nose than I for that sort of thing, and she's twice as curious and three times as reckless as I am. We can't discount the possibility that she started nosing around here and ran afoul of someone or something."

Constance relented and sent him away with a final admonition.

"Don't be gone long, and please, stay out of trouble."

Stone laughed. "What makes you think I would get into trouble?"

INTERLUDE 3

The handholds on the side of the steep cliff were few and far between. Stone tried to follow Gideon's path, but the small man scrambled up the sheer face like a spider up a wall.

"Are you a spider or a man?" Stone mumbled. For a moment, he imagined Gideon scurrying up the side of the Washington Monument, his hands and feet clinging to the smooth marble. He chuckled and kept climbing.

He reached the top and let out a groan. Gideon was picking his way across a frozen, deeply crevassed slope.

"An icefall! That is simply wonderful."

An icefall was a steep, deeply crevassed surface of a glacier, unstable and drawn inexorably downward by the pull of gravity. It was essentially a slow-moving ice waterfall. Stone had climbed one before, but not without gear. Still, he had no choice.

He made his way along the slick, irregular surface, careful not to break an ankle in one of the crevasses. He took a measure of satisfaction in the fact that Gideon was not moving much faster than he.

Stone's muscles burned. Sweat poured freely down his face and stung the corners of his eyes. The cold seemed to soak through his gloves and boots.

"He had better be leading me to the monastery," Stone grumbled.

He had made it two-thirds of the way up the slope when something came flying through the air, headed directly for him. He dodged to the left as a chunk of ice the size of a bowling ball smashed into the spot where he'd been moments before. He landed awkwardly, lost his footing, and skidded back down the slope before arresting his fall.

"Where did that come from?" he muttered.

He looked around for Gideon but there was no sight of him. Surely the small man couldn't have hurled something that size. Stone shielded his eyes against the angry glare of the sun reflected off of ice. Off to the side, he caught a glimpse of something large and dark disappearing into a crevasse.

Determined to find out what the thing was, Stone scrambled after it. With a disregard bordering on recklessness, he hopped and leaped from one shifting ice sheet to another, closing in on the spot where the figure had vanished. He had almost made it when the chunk of ice beneath his foot gave way and he plunged into a deep hole.

He braced himself for impact, but it never came. Instead, he found his descent slowed by the narrowing walls of the crevasse until he came to a halt, his feet dangling in space. He shifted and tried to twist around but he was wedged tight.

"Well, this is just great." He debated calling out for Gideon to help him. He had lost sight of the man and had no way of knowing if he was even within earshot. The idea of needing rescue twice in such a short span of time didn't appeal to him, but he might not have a choice. It was a long way up and he couldn't see any handholds.

He looked down, letting his eyes adjust to the dimness

of the crevasse. His eyes fell on the slick floor only a few feet below him. That appeared to be the likelier path.

Little by little, with lots of tearing of fabric and scouring of flesh, he managed to work his arms free of his backpack, then turn his body to the side, freeing first his shoulders, then his thighs. With his cheek pressed against the icy cold wall, he slid down until his feet touched solid ground.

The confines were still constricting and could take only tiny sips of breath as he inched his way forward. When he finally had room to move, he retrieved his pack and followed the crevasse until it opened up on a narrow mountain trail.

He took three steps and froze.

There in the snow before him was a giant footprint! It was humanlike, with a pronounced heel and ball of the foot, and five toes. He knelt to take a closer look. He estimated the print was fourteen inches long and twelve inches across at the widest point. He let out a low whistle. Oversized footprints in the snow could sometimes be explained by melting and refreezing, but this was fresh snow.

He tried to imagine the size of the person or creature that had left the print and wondered if it might have thrown the chunk of ice at him. He stood and looked around. Was it still lurking somewhere nearby.

Behind him, someone muffled a tiny cough. Stone whirled around to see Gideon standing there.

"You did well to escape back there," Gideon said. "I feared I would have to rescue you again."

"What sort of creature left this track?" Stone said brusquely, embarrassed that Gideon had managed to sneak up on him.

Gideon shook his head.

"Are you here to track beast or do you seek the monastery?"

"I'm just asking a question. I think this thing tried to kill me."

"If it wanted to kill you, you would be dead. Follow me and try to keep up."

Gideon let them around the side of the mountain and out onto a ledge that was scarcely wide enough for Stone to fit onto. Below was a drop of hundreds of feet to a rocky death.

He concentrated on maintaining his balance and taking one step at a time. His boots scarcely fit on the tight ledge. Gusts of wind battered him like invisible hands trying to send him to his death. He ought to be terrified, but as he looked out at the snow-capped mountain peaks all around him, he was overwhelmed by the beauty of the world. Up here it was easy to forget the ugly side of the human race and simply focus on the beauty of creation. A smile spread across his face.

"I have seen that look before," Gideon said. "Right before someone jumps. One easy step and all your problems go away. Are you giving up, Brock Stone?"

"Not at all," Stone said. "I've been thinking of the world as an ugly place, but really, it's quite beautiful. It's only the hearts of men that make it ugly."

Gideon did not appear to be impressed by this revelation. He quickened his pace, and by the time Stone's feet were once again on solid ground, the little man was halfway up the next slope. Stone took a gulp of thin air and resisted the urge to pick up a rock and fling it at the annoying local.

"Why did you come back for me if you're just going

to leave me behind again?" he shouted.

"I will not leave you," Gideon called back. "It is not an option."

"Some sort of code of honor?" Stone asked, resuming the climb.

"When someone speaks the name of the Celestial Master in the hearing of an initiate, the initiate must decide whether or not to kill that person. I cannot allow the mountain to kill you. That privilege will be mine and mine alone."

It was a measure of Stone's world-weariness that the declaration didn't stir any feelings within him at all. It seemed like men had been trying to kill him, and he them, since the day he enlisted, and he was still here.

"Are you planning on killing me?" Stone asked.

Gideon stopped and turned to grin at Stone.

"I have not decided yet."

11- JUNINA

Junina was a petite girl with light brown skin and long, glossy black hair which she wore in a single braid. Her downcast eyes were big and brown. Constance couldn't help but feel a pang of sympathy for this lovely young lady who seemed so sad. At first, she was friendly, but she frowned at the mention of Trinity's name.

"She asked a lot of questions," Junina said. "Asked me about things I don't like to talk about."

Constance hurriedly explained the reason for her queries. "I don't want to ask you anything personal. I am just hoping you can help me determine where she was going next."

The girl shook her head. "She didn't say. I just showed her around the school and told her what it was like to live here. Then she asked me about where I lived before." Junina started to tremble.

Constance took her by the hand. "We don't have to talk about that. Could you perhaps walk me around the building? Show me the things you showed her?"

Ward chose that moment to make an abrupt entrance. "Sorry." His tone said he was anything but. "May I help you with anything?"

Constance smiled sweetly. "As a matter of fact, you can mind the office while Junina shows me around. Mrs. Carroll's orders, you understand. Thank you so much." She considered giving him a condescending pat on the cheek, but the thought of touching the sweaty man filled her with revulsion, so she settled for taking Junina by the hand and leading her out into the hallway.

As soon as they were out the door, Junina relaxed.

"Thank you for getting me away from him. He makes me uncomfortable."

"He gives me the same feeling," Constance said. "But he doesn't scare me, and he shouldn't frighten you, either."

"It's not him I'm afraid of. It's Klaus, the caretaker. He does whatever Ward tells him to."

Constance remembered seeing the quiet conversation between the seemingly ineffectual Ward and the intimidating Klaus. Was there more at play here than a simple relationship between supervisor and employee?

"What can you tell me about Klaus?" she asked.

"A few months ago, our old caretaker suddenly retired. Didn't give a reason or say goodbye, even though he had been here for fifteen years. Klaus showed up the next day and Ward hired him on the spot."

"Any idea where he came from?"

"New York. Russia before that. That's all I know."

They wandered the halls of the old building. For the life of her, Constance could not imagine what interest Trinity would have had in the history of this place. She had held out hope for the library, but it had been converted to an infirmary, the small collection of books either donated or put in storage.

"Was there anywhere in particular that Trinity seemed especially curious about? Did she spend a lot of time in any one place?"

Junina stopped in her tracks. "There was, but it's downstairs. I don't like to go down there."

"Could you give me directions?" Constance asked.

"No, I will show you. You shouldn't be alone in case

Klaus is down there. He doesn't get too forward as long as there are others around."

As they descended the stairs to the lower level, Constance felt a rising tension. The air was cool and damp here, and the air smelled of mold. She tried to lighten the mood with casual conversation.

"Junina is a beautiful name. Is it from the Bible?" Constance couldn't believe she was babbling about name origins. This place unnerved her. A chill ran down her spine and she was forcibly reminded of the ghost stories surrounding the so-called school for insane girls.

"Junina is the name I was given when I came here. My birth name is Colestah. She was a powerful warrior and medicine woman who could speak to the spirits."

"I wouldn't mind having her around if we encounter Klaus," Constance said.

Junina managed a tiny laugh. "Your friend said something very much like that."

"Trinity is a brave woman and she takes courage from stories of women like Colestah."

"I am afraid she is too brave for her own good," Junina said.

"What do you mean by that?"

"She was asking about dark, dangerous things." Junina clenched her fists and began to shake.

Constance seized the girl by the shoulders. "Listen to me. You are exactly right. My friend has a tendency to get herself into trouble. I understand that you don't want to talk about these dark, dangerous things, but it is very important that you tell me."

"She wanted to see the cursed cellar," Junina whispered.

"And what else?" Constance asked firmly.

The young girl squeezed her eyes shut. A single tear trickled down her cheek.

"She wanted to know where I saw the hairy men."

12- THE CELLAR

Stone crept along the dark hallway. The musty air and dim lighting made this lower level feel like a basement. It took a few minutes of searching before he found a stout wooden door with the words *In Vino Veritas* carved in the polished surface. *In wine there is truth.* Stone smiled at the thought. He touched the shiny brass doorknob. It was clean and free of rust. Someone had kept the door polished. But what was the point?

Not surprisingly, the door was locked. Stone, however, was an accomplished picklock, and he had the door open in short order. He stepped inside and shut the door behind him before clicking on his flashlight.

A vaulted stone ceiling rose above him. To his left and right, wooden crates were stacked in neat piles. A beautiful mosaic depicting a bunch of grapes adorned the far wall. The space was dry and free of dust. Someone was regularly cleaning this old storage space. Stranger and stranger.

He examined the crates, walking up and down the rows, shining his light on each, but nothing leaped out at him. Perhaps it wasn't the contents of the room, but the room itself that was special. He examined the floor and the ceiling, then moved to the mosaic on the far wall. And then he saw it. Inside one of the fat, purple grapes was an eye inside a triangle. The Eye of Providence, also known as the All-Seeing Eye. It appeared on the Great Seal of the United States, but it was also a symbol of the Illuminati.

He reached out to touch it, but then he heard the soft

sound of a doorknob being turned gently. Someone on the other side of the door was trying to enter quietly. Stone clicked off his light and hurried to stand beside the door. There was nowhere else to hide. The door swung open and the electric light clicked on, bathing the cellar in rheumy light. Klaus strode inside, carrying a monkey wrench the length of Stone's forearm.

The German was no ordinary caretaker. He sensed Stone's presence immediately, and lashed out with the monkey wrench. The heavy steel missed caving in Stone's skull by inches. It took a chunk out of the wall, sending sharp bits of rock flying like shrapnel.

Stone dodged to the side but before he could attack, Klaus whipped the wrench around in a powerful backswing aimed at Stone's chest. The blow missed, leaving the German open for a sharp kick to the groin and a solid right cross to the chin. The combination would have sent most men to their knees, but Klaus only grunted and took a step back before swinging the wrench again. Stone saw it coming. He dodged the blow, then drove his fist into the back of Klaus's elbow. He caught the man in the perfect spot, causing the nerves in his hand to go temporarily numb and forcing him to drop the monkey wrench.

It hit the ground with a loud clang. Klaus dove for it, but Stone managed to kick it away. It skittered across the smooth floor and out the door. Better that neither of them had it than the beastly German get his hands on it again.

As Klaus clambered back to his feet, Stone aimed a roundhouse kick at the man's head. Klaus raised his arm to block the kick. Stone's foot struck a slab of muscle so dense it was like kicking a tree trunk. Klaus let out a beastly roar and tried to tackle Stone around the waist.

Stone managed to escape the giant man's powerful clutches, but now found himself circling away, trying to figure out how to disable this behemoth.

He struck with the flat of his hand and poked Klaus in the eye. It was a cruel blow, one that could blind the big man. But, the German had just tried to turn Stone's skull into pulp, so he didn't feel too guilty about it. Klaus cried out in pain and instinctively put his hands to his face. Stone kicked him hard in the kidney. Klaus froze for a second, then his knees buckled. Stone seized the advantage, battering the big German with fists, feet, and elbows. Klaus reeled. Stone drew back his fist to throw a hard right cross.

White light flashed and a loud boom filled Stone's ears. It took him a second to realize Klaus had punched him.

"Gosh all Potomac!" he said, habitually uttering one of the few swears his mother had tolerated during his teen years. No one had ever punched him that hard. He took a step back, and shook his head.

Klaus stood hunched over in front of the door. His fists were clenched and hate burned in his eyes. But he still had some fight left in him.

"What are you?" Stone asked.

A grin split the big man's face. "I am an Aryan. You will not leave this place alive."

"What is Ward hiding down here?"

The German's only answer was a simian bellow. He sprang forward with surprising agility and crashed into Stone. The two big men smashed into a pile of crates, shattering them. Old, dusty papers spilled over Stone's head. Another falling crate spilled out china and a kerosene oil lamp someone had not bothered to empty.

The contents splashed all over Klaus.

Stone saw his chance. He headbutted the bigger man across the bridge of his nose and shoved him away just long enough for Stone to pull his Zippo from his pocket and flick it on.

"Here, catch." He tossed the lighter to Klaus, who stared at it dumbly for a few seconds even after the kerosene on his arms caught fire.

Klaus let out an angry shout but he didn't run or try to extinguish the flames. Instead, he resumed his attack. A fiery fist just missed Stone's chin. Stone returned a right cross that buckled the German's knees. His eyes rolled back and he slumped to the ground. Stone was surprised to see Constance standing behind him, holding the monkey wrench in both hands.

"I think I got him." She stared blankly at the fallen man, the golden light of burning crates flickering off her fair skin.

"Well done. Now, let's get out of here before this whole place goes up." Stone seized her by the elbow and took a step toward the door only to see it slam shut.

Constance began to cough as acrid smoke filled the air. "What are we going to do?"

"I'll break it down." Stone stepped back to take a run at it.

And then a burning shelf crashed down against the door, sealing them inside.

13- THE SECRET ROOM

Stone grabbed Constance and pulled her out of the way as another stack of burning crates fell. The air was thick with smoke and he could barely see her. His eyes watered and his throat and lungs burned with every breath.

"It must have been Ward!" Constance coughed. "He's closed us in here to die."

"I've got an idea. Come on." Stone peered through the thickening smoke and found his way to the back wall where he'd been inspecting the odd mosaic tile. When they reached it, he clicked on his flashlight and shone it on the bunch of grapes.

"Find the grape with the All-Seeing Eye on it!"

As mad as that must have sounded, Constance didn't question him. She spotted it right away.

"It's right here!" She blinked away the water in her eyes, looked again, then glanced up at Stone. "It's a perfect circle and it's recessed."

"Push it and see what happens."

"Ordinarily I wouldn't let a man get away with saying that to me, but considering present circumstances…" She pressed her thumb to the circle. As Stone had hoped, it sank into the wall, and then the mosaic swung back, opening into a dark space beyond. "A secret door!"

They hurried through and shut the door behind them.

The beam of Stone's flashlight swept across a hospital bed and an array of vials, tubes, and needles.

"Is this some kind of laboratory?" Constance asked, moving closer to inspect one of the vials.

"I wouldn't say a lab. No one has been cooking anything up in here. But it looks like a patient has been receiving care."

"The sort of care you wouldn't want the rest of the staff to know about." Constance held the vial up and Stone shone his light on it. It contained a drop of viscous, emerald green liquid. "I think we should hold on to this." She stoppered it and tucked it into her pocket.

"I wonder if Trinity found this place?" Stone said. And then a dark thought entered his mind. "Ward!" He pounded his fist in his palm. White-hot rage burned inside of him. "If he has Trinity, I'll…"

"Calm down. He doesn't have her."

"How do you know that?"

"Because Junina saw her leave. She also told me why Trinity came here and where she was going next. And it sounds like it has nothing to do with whatever all of this is."

"What's the story, then?"

Constance flashed a crooked smile and quirked her eyebrow. "I'll tell you after you find us a way out of here."

There was a back door, which they managed to open by application of brute force. The encounter left Stone's shoulder smarting and his ears ringing from the protest of the hinges.

They walked and sometimes crawled forty yards along a muddy, foul-smelling tunnel. It came to an end at the bottom of an old well. Rusty iron rungs set in the stone ran up into the darkness.

"I suppose this is the way out," Stone said.

"You will go first," Constance said.

"Good idea. I'll go up and make sure the rungs are going to hold."

Constance gaped at him as if he were addled in the brain. "That is not the reason."

Stone scratched his head. "All right, then. What is your reason?"

"It is because I am wearing a dress."

Stone couldn't help but laugh. "I will never understand women."

"That is the wisest thing you have ever said to me." Constance patted him on the cheek. "Now, get us out of here."

Stone began climbing, careful to test each rung before putting his full weight on it. Though the bars were old and pitted, they held. Rung by rung, he ascended until he reached the top, where a stone slab barred their way. He tested its weight. It was heavy, but he thought he could move it, assuming, of course, the rungs which supported his weight continued to hold. And then he heard something on the other side. A voice!

"What did you find?" Constance called.

"Quiet! I hear something out there."

"Don't order me to be quiet!" Constance whispered.

Stone didn't reply. He listened. The voice came again.

"There, I done it. You owe me a silver dollar."

"The wager was an hour in the haunted graveyard. You have three more minutes," another voice replied.

Relief flooded through Brock Stone, followed by a flare of mischievous intent. With a powerful shove he heaved the stone cover aside.

"Who disturbs my rest?" he bellowed.

Terrified shrieks filled the air. Stone thrust his head out to see Alex and Moses fleeing through the graveyard. He threw back his head and let out a hearty laugh.

"That was unkind." Constance had climbed up and waited a couple of rungs below him.

"An opportunity like that comes once in a lifetime. I couldn't help myself," Stone admitted. "But at least we know Alex is as frightened of ghosts as Moses is."

"Men. You're just large children, aren't you?"

"Sometimes." Stone clambered out of the hole and gave Constance a hand. "But I'm serious when I need to be."

"Believe me, I've noticed. I'm just happy to see that Trinity was wrong about one thing."

"What thing would that be?" he asked.

"Trinity always says you have no discernible sense of humor."

14- AVALANCHE!

The truck bounced along the rough mountain road, climbing higher into the Cascade Mountains. From his seat on the covered bed, Moses let out an angry shout and pounded his fist on the back of the cab. Since the joke Stone had pulled on his friends, Moses had refused to ride in the cab with the others. That would change if the low-hanging gray clouds finally cut loose.

"Sorry!" Stone called to his friend. "Nothing I can do about the condition of the road."

"You could at least slow down for the worst of the bumps and ruts," Alex grumbled. He too had been in a foul mood since leaving the girls' school.

"You recall it was Constance and I who were nearly murdered, today? All you got was soiled shorts."

"I did not soil my shorts," Alex grumbled.

"You shouldn't fret," Constance said, patting Alex on the knee. "Anyone would be frightened if something popped up out of a tomb like that."

"Not frightened so much as startled." Alex didn't meet her eye.

Out of the corner of his eye, Stone saw something move in the trees off to the right, heading toward them. He hit the brakes and the truck skidded to a halt in a cloud of dust.

Something huge and covered in brown hair trotted out onto the narrow dirt road. His heart skipped a beat. As the dust cleared, he finally got a good look at what barred their path.

"It's gorgeous," Constance gasped.

It was a huge bull elk, standing at least eight feet at the shoulder. Each antler must have been three feet long. It barely registered their presence as it crossed the road and moved off into the trees on the other side.

"Sure wish I had my rifle right now," Moses said.

"You would not destroy a beautiful creature like that!" Constance exclaimed.

"You can bet your bottom dollar I would. That's a whole lot of meat."

The elk trotted away. In a matter of seconds, it had vanished from sight.

"Makes you think, doesn't it?" Alex said.

"About what?" Constance said.

"How quickly something can vanish from sight out here. Or could remain hidden if it wanted to."

"Quit trying to put a scare into me," Moses said.

The roar of the engine drowned out Alex's retort as Stone got the truck back in motion. As he drove, his eyes searched the forest. Alex wasn't wrong. The elk had melted into the forest in an instant. This was not the domain of man, but of the creatures of the wild.

They wound along the narrow road and eventually emerged high on a steep mountainside. Here, logging had cleared away much of the forest. There would be nothing to arrest their fall should they leave the road.

Stone felt tension rising among his companions as they drove along mere inches from certain death. The dirt road was little more than a downward sloping dirt path. Without the protection of the trees, the elements had gradually washed it away. He glanced over and saw Constance holding Alex's hand, her knuckles white from the tight grip she had on him.

"It will be fine," Stone said, just as the rear wheels briefly lost traction and the truck fishtailed.

Constance let out a shriek.

"We're all right," Stone said.

"Up there!" Constance pointed up the slope. "Look out!"

Stone's heart skipped a beat as he looked up to see a wall of boulders and logs bounding down on them like a cavalry charge. An avalanche! Knowing it was only a matter of seconds before the truck was knocked off the road and sent tumbling down the mountainside, Stone floored it.

The wheels spun on the hard-packed dirt before catching. The truck lurched forward and gradually gained speed. They hit a bump in the rough dirt road, the vehicle went airborne, sending an icy flutter through Stone's gut. It hit the ground with an impact Stone felt from the base of his spine all the way to the tip of his skull. The truck bounced and the front passenger side wheel slid off the edge of the road.

Alex called out a warning and Constance let out a curse suitable for any soldier or sailor Stone had ever met. He maintained his calm and resisted the urge to overcorrect. The truck seemed to tip to the side. The drop seemed even more precipitous.

"Stone?" Alex said nervously.

Stone didn't reply. Focusing on the task at hand, he managed to get all four wheels back on the narrow road. But they weren't out of danger yet.

The avalanche was almost upon them!

Stone gritted his teeth and kept the pedal to the metal. The engine roared and the truck flew forward. The tumbling boulders and debris had kicked up a cloud of dust in their wake. It looked like a wall of death closing in on them.

Twenty feet.

Ten feet.

"We're not going to make it!" Constance cried.

A boulder the size of Stone's head flew through the air, hurtling right at them. Stone braced himself. Everything seemed to happen in slow motion. Alex shouted, Constance swore, rubble closed in on them. Safety loomed just up ahead where the road wound back into the shelter of the forest. They zoomed past the flying boulder with only feet to spare.

"Thank heaven!" Constance breathed.

And then something struck the rear of the truck and drove the rear wheels off the road. The truck tilted wildly, the wheels spun, trying to find traction. They slid and fishtailed as Stone fought to keep the vehicle from tumbling down the hill. They finally came to a stop just short of the forest. Behind them, the avalanche rolled along twenty feet from their rear bumper.

"That was close." Alex closed his eyes and threw his head back. The motion caused the truck to tilt downhill.

"Hold still!" Stone warned. "We're teetering on a knife's edge here!" He assessed the situation. The truck was partway off the road. At the moment, they were perfectly balanced. But too much of a shift one way or the other and they would be in trouble. They would need to proceed with caution.

"What do you want me to do, Stone?" Moses shouted.

Stone glanced back to see his friend lying splayed out across the truck bed.

"Carefully pull yourself toward the uphill side."

Moses did as he was instructed, shifting his full weight

to the uphill side of the truck. Stone felt a slight shifting of the weight distribution, but their situation remained precarious.

"Constance, you climb onto my lap."

The young woman's cheeks went scarlet. "I absolutely will not!"

"We need to get your and Alex's weight on this side of the truck."

Constance appeared to debate this for a moment. Then she gave an affirmative nod. "Alex can sit on your lap." Alex sputtered and protested, but Constance shushed him. "You are heavier than I. It will make for better balance."

"Don't you dare say she's right," Alex warned Stone. "Matter of fact, just don't say anything at all." His face as red as his hair as he clambered, crablike, over Constance, then shifted onto Stone's lap. Alex was much too tall for his legs to fit below the steering wheel, so he settled for lying across Stone's lap with his knees pulled to his chest and his head and shoulders stuck out the driver's side window.

Finally, with the weight better distributed, Stone was able to get the truck back onto the road. Alex wasted no time scrambling back to his seat where he stared balefully out the passenger window. Stone was also eager to forget the entire incident.

"It's a good thing you saw that landslide coming," he said to Constance. "Without your warning, we would have been swept away."

"Yes, that was well done," Alex said, obviously relieved to have something else to talk about. "You really saved our skins."

Constance looked down, bit her lip. "I have a

confession to make. I didn't actually see the avalanche. I cried out because I saw a huge, hairy man moving in the trees."

INTERLUDE 4

May, 1927
Five Years Ago

Stone and Gideon took shelter in a small cave. The sun was setting, and the air was growing frigid. It must have been a regular stopping place for people traversing the mountain because a small store of firewood had been laid aside. Stone built a small fire, then shared his trail rations with his new companion.

Gideon took out a small flask and took a sip. He closed his eyes and let out a small sigh of contentment. The corners of his mouth twitched in a tiny smile. Finally, he held the flask out to Stone.

Stone caught a whiff of strong liquor, minty with a hint of juniper. He seldom imbibed but didn't mind taking a drink when courtesy demanded it. This seemed like one of those times.

He took a sip. It burned on the way down but filled his stomach with a pleasantly warm sensation. He felt his stiff, sore muscles relax.

"What did you mean when you said you 'needed something to believe in again'?" Gideon said.

The subject was an uncomfortable one but if Stone expected Gideon to help him, he owed the man an explanation.

"I am... was a soldier. I enlisted from a desire to protect people." He paused, gazed into the flames. "Soon they began sending me on special missions. Sometimes I

"I can show you right now, if you are willing."

"I am."

Gideon opened a drawstring pouch and poured a handful of white, sparkling powder into his palm.

"The first Treasure is the Treasure of Salt."

The stuff in Gideon's hand didn't look like salt. It reflected the firelight in a wide spectrum of colors.

"Do you truly wish to see the monastery and gain the Five Treasures?" Gideon intoned. It sounded like part of a ritual.

"Absolutely."

"Do you vow to complete this journey, no matter the cost?"

Stone didn't hesitate. Something in his life had to change.

"I give you my word."

Without warning, Gideon flung the powder into Stone's eyes. Stone let out a shout. Instinctively he threw a punch at Gideon, but he was weak, and his movements were sluggish. The liquor had done its work.

He felt Gideon grab him by the wrists. Stone has no strength left to fight.

Gideon whispered in his ear.

"To be born again, first you must die."

Darkness swallowed him.

15- ROCKMIRE

Rockmire was a small logging town. Truth be told, it was barely a town at all. A combination filling station and country store stood on one side of the dirt road. Across the street was an establishment called the Woodsman's Complaint. A hand-painted sign out front advertised soda pop, but the man who came staggering out the door had obviously been drinking something stronger.

Stone wasn't all that surprised. Prohibition was growing increasingly unpopular and seemed likely to be repealed in the coming years. Already, many jurisdictions were turning a blind eye at speakeasies, provided the establishments were discreet and made generous donations to the local powers that be. Was the revenue department really going to send an agent into the Cascades to try and stop a town full of lumberjacks and hunters from having a drink? Stone wasn't a heavy drinker by any stretch, but he thought a grown man ought to be able to decide such things for himself. *And a woman.* He heard Trinity's voice inside his head, and it made him smile.

A few cabins stood nearby. One of them was larger than the others and the sign outside proclaimed it to be a boarding house.

They pulled up to the filling station and were pleasantly surprised to see that the owners were apparently happy to do business with anybody. As Stone was parking the truck, they saw a black man exit the store, chatting amiably with a Yakama Indian and a white man.

They clambered into the back of a truck driven by a Chinese fellow and drove off. Stone saw Moses gaping at the truck as it disappeared.

"You thinking about moving West?" Stone asked.

Moses grinned and shook his head. "Virginia is home. I just wish it loved me as much as I love it."

Stone couldn't think of anything useful to say. He gave a sad nod and inclined his head toward the store.

"Let's go inside. I'll buy you a Coca Cola."

"You think they have that out here?" Moses asked.

"I had one at the Amsterdam Olympics, and that was a few years ago. Surely they have it out here."

"You were at the Amsterdam Olympics?" Alex asked.

"Not officially. Actually, forget I told you that."

Alex rolled his eyes. "You know I hate it when you do that."

The shop owners were a couple named Vince and Deb. They were polite, but seemed uncertain what to make of these newcomers. Sensing their discomfort, the men browsed the store while Constance engaged the couple in casual conversation. She asked about the town and learned that Deb owned the boarding house, which was currently filled to capacity with married loggers and their families. Most loggers lived at the logging camps and only ventured into town for supplies or a drink at the saloon.

When Constance asked if the couple had seen Trinity, the air grew thick with tension.

"She came in here a couple of times, but she didn't talk," Vince said.

"Knowing Trinity, I find that difficult to believe," Constance said. "At minimum, she would have peppered you with friendly questions until you felt like you'd been turned inside out."

Vince flashed a smile. "I only meant that she didn't say much about herself."

"She has gone missing and we're trying to find her," Constance said. "Do you have any idea where she might have gone?"

Watching from the far side of the store, Stone saw the couple exchange nervous glances. They knew something but were reluctant to say.

"Please," he said, approaching the front counter. "I appreciate that you are respecting her privacy but we need your help."

Deb did a double-take, then relaxed. "I know your face. You are her fellow, Rocky Smith, something like that?"

"Brock Stone, and I'm surprised she called me her fellow."

"My words, not hers. She showed me a photo of you. Said you were not as bright as you are handsome."

"Truer words have never been spoken," Alex chimed in.

"You calling him handsome?" Moses said.

"No. I mean, oh never mind." Alex marched up to the counter, paid for his soda pop, and drank it in silence while Deb and Vince filled them in on what they knew about Trinity.

"She seems like a bright girl, a bit hard-headed. I like her," Vince said.

Deb turned and frowned. "Since when have you liked hard-headed women?"

Vince cocked his head, frowned, and then his shoulders sagged beneath his wife's stern gaze.

"How about I let you tell the story?" he said.

"I think that would be for the best. Have a Coca Cola, dear." Deb patted her husband on the shoulder and gave him a gentle shove toward the drink cooler. "You'll have to excuse him. The storm last week wiped out most of his herb garden."

"About Trinity?" Constance prompted.

"Like you said, she asks a lot of questions, so many in fact that it's hard to know which answers she's actually interested in. She stopped in a few times, visited the saloon at least once. She slept at the boarding house, but usually came in late and left early."

"Did you get any sense of what she was actually investigating?" Constance asked.

"Judging by what I've heard from people who come into the store, not that I asked, mind you, she was interested in two things: local logging business, and the Bigfoot."

"The what?" Moses asked.

"The Indians call him Sasquatch. He's a big, hairy ape man who lives in the mountains."

"Have you seen this giant ape man?" Moses asked.

Deb shrugged. "I've never gotten a good look at him, but I've seen things moving through the forest that aren't any known creature that lives out here. And trust me, I'm no tenderfoot."

"But she never told us which lumber camps she was investigating, or where she might have gone to look for a Bigfoot," Vince said.

"I thought I was telling the story." Deb hooked a thumb in the direction of her husband. "What he just said."

"If you were hunting a Bigfoot, where would you look?" Stone asked.

"I wouldn't," Deb said flatly. "I'm not joking about that. Even if it doesn't exist, this wilderness alone is too much for most people."

"I understand," Stone assured her. "I wouldn't be here if it weren't important."

"It's just not something we get into," Deb said. "If customers mention it, we pretend to listen out of politeness."

"How about the logging camps?" Stone asked. "Do you know if any of them are owned by a man named Kane?"

"Didn't know that name when your friend asked me, and it still doesn't ring a bell," Deb said. "I'm sorry, but I really can't tell you anything else. She hasn't been around in several days. Her room was empty, so we figured whatever business she had out here, she was finished with it."

"She only left behind the book she borrowed from me," Vince offered.

"What book was that?" Constance asked.

"A book about Lewis and Clark. There's a rumor that they discovered a treasure cave in these parts. Miss Paige was quite interested."

"I think she was being polite," Deb said.

Vince ignored her, but the twinkle in his eye said he had not missed her rejoinder. "I told her about a spot not far from here where Lewis and Clark made camp." He paused, scratched his chin. "Come to think of it, she asked if there was a lumber camp near there, and I told her that Davis and his outfit have set up on that very site."

Stone smiled. Finally, a lead!

"Be careful around Davis and his outfit, if that's where you're headed," Deb warned.

"Why is that?" Stone asked.

"Almost everyone around here gets along fairly well. We're all in the same boat, cutting down trees for a living or making a living off the people who do the cutting. But Davis and his crew, they're just different. They're standoffish, and they don't hire locals. And those Germans that work with them." She shivered. "I can't put my finger on it, but they aren't right. I hope your friend didn't run afoul of them. We truly did believe she had left town."

"Hopefully she has," Constance said. "Thank you for your help."

Alex was waiting for them beside the truck. "What's the plan, boss?"

"I think it's time we split up. We've got two clear lines of inquiry. One is Kane's lumber camp, which seems to coincide with the Lewis and Clark clue from Trinity's note. Moses and I will follow up on that one."

"Which leaves us to ask around about Bigfoot," Alex groaned.

"Look on the bright side," Constance said. "You get to spend the evening in the company of an intelligent woman."

"Both women and intelligence are in short supply at our hose, so that sounds lovely." Arm in arm, they headed across the street to the speakeasy.

16- THE LUMBER CAMP AGAIN

Stone ignored the stares as he and Moses strode into the logging camp. In any event, he doubted many of the looks were for him. Unlike the other lumberjacks he'd seen in Rockmire, there was not a brown face among this crew.

Wood smoke hung low in the damp air, carrying an acrid scent to his nostrils. Over the years he'd developed heightened senses, which was not always a pleasant thing. Beneath the smoke and the damp, earthy smell hung the foul aroma of human habitation: body odor, cheap whiskey, tobacco smoke, and the reek of a nearby latrine. He ignored it all, keeping his eyes trained on a big, blond man who sat on a stump, drinking from a tin cup.

The man's eyes widened as he spotted the newcomers. The fellow stood, his gaze uncertain. This was Davis, the foreman.

"You two lost?"

"We're right where we intended to be," Stone said. "I'll make this brief. We're looking for a friend." He described Trinity, and saw a spark of recognition in the man's eyes.

"I don't…" Davis started to shake his head, but froze beneath Stone's icy glare. "I don't know where she is," he amended. "She did stop by about five days back, maybe a week? Said she was a reporter."

was required to kill people, and I had only the assurance of those above me that my targets constituted a threat to our national security. Sometimes the danger the person posed was obvious. Most of the time I had no idea how my actions fit into the larger picture. That was difficult for me. But recently…" He couldn't put his thoughts into words, so he took another sip of liquor.

"Allow me to speculate." Gideon took the flask from him and capped it. "You discovered that in practice, what is good for the country often means what is good for the bank accounts of politicians and their donors."

"Spot on," Stone said. "I realized I was a weapon fired by others. Some of us used that as an excuse to rationalize our actions, others simply didn't care. But I can't deny that I have a conscience and free will. I had no control over the decisions my superiors made, but the decision to reenlist was mine alone."

"I take it you did not?"

Stone shook his head.

"I need perspective. These days I have a hard time telling the good guys from the bad." He barked a rueful laugh."

"In the womb, we are all sightless," Gideon said. "It is only at the moment of our birth that our eyes are truly opened, and our view of the world begins to take shape."

"Does that mean I've been in the womb all these years?" Stone took another drink. Fatigue was creeping up on him.

"In a way. But it is possible to be reborn with all of your eyes opened."

"What does that mean?"

"It is the first of the Five Treasures."

"Can you show me the way?" Stone's heart raced.

"What was she inquiring about?" Stone asked.

"Deaths. Well, the rumors of deaths. It's all a bunch of lies, though. This is a safe camp." Davis's gaze flicked up and to the side and he blinked several times before continuing. "I answered her questions and she left. Said she was going back to Washington. DC."

"Maybe the ape men got her," a burly blond-haired man rumbled in a heavy German accent. Several of the lumberjacks let out raucous laughs.

"Shut your mouths," Davis snapped.

The men ignored their foreman, and continued to laugh, but fell silent under Stone's cold stare. He turned back to Davis.

"I need your help." His tone said it was anything but a request.

Davis looked around at his men, then nodded. "Walk with me." He put his hands in his pockets and walked out of camp at a relaxed gait, as if he were out for an evening stroll. When they were out of earshot, he finally spoke.

"The townsfolk are always trying to blame their troubles on us. But it's their women who are disappearing, not our lumberjacks."

"Missing women?" Stone asked.

"A few women have gone missing and some of the drunks in the saloon blame it on Bigfoot." He made a face to show what he thought of the idea.

"What do you think happened to them?"

"I know for a fact that one of them made off with a lumberjack, skin as dark as this fellow here." He inclined his head in Moses's direction. "Her old man is too ashamed to admit it. He'd rather people think she made off with an ape man." Davis forced a grin.

"You haven't had a single man vanish?" Stone asked.

"That's why I wanted to speak to you in private. We did have one man disappear a few months back. I told the men that a company man had taken him away. They do that from time to time. The truth is, he wandered off one day and was never heard from again. The men are so superstitious about Bigfoot, and the Indians have been filling their heads with stories about sightings in the area where Klaus disappeared."

"What did he look like?" Stone asked.

"Like a bear with mange. Huge German, reddish brown hair everywhere but on his head." Davis frowned. "Why do you ask?"

"When I was in Seattle I met a man by that name who fits the description to a T. You don't know a man named Ward, do you?"

Davis flinched, then froze beneath Stone's cold stare. After a silent second, he cleared his throat. "Never heard of him. Now, I need to be getting back. I hope you find your girl. She's a pretty one."

Stone knew the man was hiding something, but at the moment there was nothing to be gained from further questions. He would have to conduct his own investigation.

"Thanks for your time. You might see me again." He shook the man's hand, giving it an unnecessary squeeze. Davis winced, but whether it was from the handshake or the thought of Stone coming back, who could say?

17 – THE WOODSMAN'S COMPLAINT

The Woodsman's Complaint was even worse than Alex had expected. The tables and chairs were mismatched and the wooden floor needed sweeping, not to mention a good mopping. He crinkled his nose as he caught a whiff of stale beer and urine. He felt immediately out of place, but it was all the town of Rockmire had to offer.

"I regret I can't take you somewhere nicer for our first date." He immediately felt his cheeks grow hot and he forced a laugh.

"You can make it up to me when we return to civilization. And by that, I mean D.C., not Seattle." She patted his cheek sweetly. "Besides, we are here for information, not to soak up the atmosphere."

"True enough. I suppose we'll have to drink something. I doubt the glasses are clean."

A rough-hewn bar ran along the wall to the right. Behind it, a sagging bookcase held an assortment of liquor. A sallow-faced bartender scowled at Alex and Constance as they approached. The man was burly with silver-speckled black hair and pale skin.

"Can I get you something?" the man grunted.

"I don't suppose you have red wine?" Constance asked.

The bartender smirked, then reached below the bar and pulled out a bottle with no label. "We don't get much call for this around here, but it's good stuff. Straight from Napa Valley."

"We'll take the bottle." Alex grossly overpaid and winced when the bartender handed them a pair of chipped mugs.

The bartender quirked an eyebrow. "Sorry, we broke all the wine glasses in the last brawl."

"No worries." Alex chose a table in the middle of the room and waited while Constance poured.

"The wine is not going to breathe properly in this." She cast a baleful stare at her mug.

"It's all about surface area," Alex said. "Just keep swirling it. It amounts to the same."

Constance's brow furrowed and she gave her drink a tentative swirl. "I feel foolish."

"It's not foolish, it's science." Alex laughed. "We're sitting in a lumberjack bar drinking red wine. We already appear foolish."

Constance laughed and raised her cup of wine. "To your very good health."

They clinked mugs and Alex grinned. Constance was a lovely lady, but an enigma. She'd kept her distance during their cross-country trip, quiet and circumspect. He wanted to get past the small talk and really get to know her. Perhaps a few drinks would put her at ease.

He raised the mug to his nostrils, inhaling the scents of dark cherry, spice, and vanilla. He took a sip and held the wine in his mouth for a few seconds, savoring the dark, fruity flavor.

"I taste licorice," Constance said. "Perhaps a touch of black pepper?"

"You know your wines."

Constance gave a small shrug and looked around. "Not a fan of decor, are they?" she observed.

Alex looked around. The walls were largely bare, save for a missing person poster hung near the door. It showed a smiling young woman with dark eyes and hair. For a moment, he thought the person on the poster was Trinity but quickly realized the resemblance was only passing.

Constance turned and followed the direction of his stare. She blanched. "That's frightening."

Alex nodded. He took another sip of his wine and inspected the room. Gathering information would not be an easy task. Neither he nor Constance fitted in.

"We should have ordered beer," he muttered.

Constance nodded. "At least we're getting lots of attention. I only hope it's the right sort."

Several men stared in their direction. Alex assumed they were ogling Constance. He let his right hand drift casually down to the lump in his pocket where he carried his Remington Model 95 Double Derringer. The pocket pistol, with its three-inch double barrel, was easy to conceal but not very accurate. He hoped he wouldn't have to use it.

A bear of a man, beady eyes peeking out from shaggy auburn hair and full beard and mustache, stood and swaggered over to the table. Alex forced a pleasant smile, ready to draw his weapon in an instant.

"I don't mean to be rude." The man's breath stank of whiskey. "But I've never seen anybody with a hook for a hand. How the hell did you manage that?"

Alex relaxed. "Believe it or not, my hand was bitten off. I was in the jungle with a friend of mine, and things went wrong. I don't think I've ever moved my getaway sticks so fast." He glanced down at his long legs.

"You an explorer?" the man asked.

"We're writers," Constance said, using the story they had concocted.

"What are you writing about out here?"

"Missing women," Alex said. "Any idea what happened to the woman in the poster?"

"No." The man grimaced. "I haven't been here long. My name's Bart. I'm an Okie."

Alex nodded. Okies were migrant workers from Oklahoma who had come west looking for better opportunities.

"Lumberjack work?"

"That's all I could find," Bart said. "I'd never cut down a tree before I came here, but I'm learning."

Alex nodded. "Is it dangerous?"

"It can be. The only bad accident I've seen was a fellow who started drinking the hooch early in the morning. I don't know what exactly happened, but he was gone that day."

"Fired?"

Bart shrugged. "I suppose. He must not have liked it too much because he just left all his stuff behind and took off."

"Interesting." Alex remembered the newspaper man's tale of rumors that lumber camp employees had been killed and their deaths covered up. But if an employer wanted to create the illusion that someone had walked off the job, why not dispose of the man's possessions?

"I've heard some odd stories since we arrived,"

Constance said. "About…" Her eyes darted back and forth, then she leaned forward and whispered. "…ape men."

The man frowned, but then he threw back his head and laughed. "Don't let that frighten you. Seems like everyone around here has a monster story to tell. Foolishness, if you ask me. Something to pass the time."

"So, you've never seen a hairy ape man?" Constance's eyes were wide, as if she were afraid, but Alex could tell it was a ruse.

"Not a one. But if it's stories you're after, old Milton could tell you one or two…or thirty." He nodded in the direction of a gray-haired man who sat alone in the corner, nursing a drink and frowning in the general direction of the other bar patrons.

"He doesn't look too friendly," Constance said.

"He's just in a bad mood because he lost all his money in a poker game about an hour ago. He's been nursing that beer ever since. Buy him a couple of rounds and he'll be your best friend. At least until his glass is empty."

They thanked the man, who took one long, last look at Alex's hook, and a longer look at Constance, before returning to his drinking mates. They decided that Constance would be the first to approach Milton. She headed to the bar, bought two beers, and made her way over to the old man, who grinned at her like Christmas had come early. After a brief exchange, she beckoned for Alex to join them.

"This is my friend, Alex," she said. "Alex, this is Milton."

Alex shook hands with Milton. The old man's grip was strong, his hand calloused. "A pleasure."

"Thanks for the drink." Milton raised his glass in

mock salute, then took a long pull. "Ah, that takes the edge off. I didn't have the luckiest night with the cards."

"Sorry to hear that," Alex said.

Milton waved the words away. "It's nothing. I get paid again in two days. I'll just be short on drinking money until then."

"Perhaps we could help you out," Constance said. "We're writers, and we understand you have stories to tell. We'd be happy to buy a few more rounds in exchange for your knowledge of certain local legends."

"As a matter of fact, I can tell you a few stories about the ape men." Milton drained his beer, set the glass on the table, and gave Alex a meaningful look.

"Let me buy you another round," Alex said. He headed to the bar and returned with two, anticipating Milton would want sufficient lubrication for his storytelling engine.

The old man thanked him and launched into his tale.

"The Indians around here have stories about ape men going back as far as they can remember. They have different names for them, but most of us call them Bigfoot or Sasquatch."

"That sounds Indian," Constance said.

Milton scratched his head. "Depends on who you listen to. I've heard it's an Indian word, and I've also heard that a white man made it up. The way the story goes, he was a teacher who collected the natives' stories about the ape men, and supposedly Sasquatch is a name that's sort of a blend of the various names for the creature."

"What do these stories tell us about this big-footed creature?" Constance asked.

"For the most part, the Indians talk about Bigfoot as if he's just another type of human, maybe a primitive ancestor. They say he catches fish, eats berries and nuts, prefers to be left alone."

"Sounds like my grandpa," Alex said.

Milton laughed. "There's worse sorts of people out there. Anyhow, the Indians kept their distance from the Sasquatch, who they said made for dangerous enemies if you angered them."

Alex nodded, keeping his silence and permitting the old man to continue.

"Luckily, they don't seem to anger too easily. They shy away from you. Most people don't even see them. Maybe hear them moving away in the forest, or catch a whiff of them." He grimaced and fanned his nose.

"But either of those things could be explained by other animals, couldn't they?" Constance asked. "Plenty of creatures have a foul odor or make noises in the woods."

Milton raised his chin, looked at the woman through slitted eyes. For a moment Alex feared the man would declare their conversation at an end, but finally, he made a thoughtful nod.

"True, but other creatures don't leave giant, almost human-looking footprints, do they?"

"Have you seen any of the footprints?" Alex asked.

"A few." Milton took a drink.

Constance nodded. "How big are these creatures?"

"Nine feet tall," Milton said. "At least, the biggest ones are. Some are smaller, but those might be the female of the species."

"What's your theory about them?" Alex asked. "What do you think they are?"

Milton shrugged. "Some sort of close relative to humans, I'd say."

"Not an ape?" Alex pressed.

"No. Otherwise they'd have no need to take the women." Milton's eyes suddenly went wide. His cheeks turned scarlet.

"What was that?" Constance asked.

"Nothing. Just the drink talking." Milton took a long swig of beer.

"Please," Constance pressed. "My friend is missing. We need to find out what happened to her, and we'll consider every possibility."

An anticipatory silence hung between them as Milton stared at the table, slowly shaking his head. Finally, he let out a huff of breath, shoulders sagging.

"It's just folk tales, but supposedly the Bigfoot kidnap human women from time to time. I don't buy into it, but whenever a woman up and disappears anywhere in the Pacific Northwest, outside of the big city, that is, somebody will blame it on the creatures."

"Have many women disappeared?" Alex asked.

"Not really. But there have been two in this area recently. Three, counting your friend. It's strange. Neither one of them was the sort to run around or take off."

Alex leaned in close, lowered his voice. "Do you think the lumber camps could have had anything to do with it?"

Milton tensed and his eyes shot toward a table in the corner where two large men in flannel shirts sat. The pair were staring in their direction. "Best not to talk like that in public. Even quietly. But maybe. I don't know."

Alex nodded. "Is there anything else you can tell us? Anything at all?"

"No." Milton shook his head. The mention of the lumber camps had flipped his personality on its head. "That's all I can tell you."

"Please! Did Trinity speak with you?" Constance asked plaintively.

Milton nodded.

"What did you tell her?" Constance laid a hand on Milton's arm. "She could be in danger."

Milton's shoulders sagged.

"She was interested in stories about the Lewis and Clark expedition. Nothing factual, mind you. She wanted legends and conspiracy theories."

Alex nodded. Growing up in the D.C. area, he'd heard a few tall tales surrounding the expedition. "What did you tell her?" he asked.

Milton took a drink, thought for a moment, then launched into his story.

"Thomas Jefferson had big dreams for the West. He expected Lewis and Clark to find everything from gold mines to woolly mammoths. But the craziest thing he wanted them to find was a lost civilization of white men." He paused to enjoy the looks of surprise on their faces.

"That's a story I want to hear," Constance said.

"It's a strange tale. In 1170, a Welsh prince Madoc set sail for North America on a voyage of discovery."

"Did you say Murdock?" Alex asked.

"I think he said Maddock," Constance said.

"Anyhow, *Madoc*," Milton said loudly, emphasizing the long *A*, "returned years later with glowing reports of his discoveries. Among the things he brought back was a breastplate made from a precious metal he called orichalcum."

"I've never heard of it," Constance said.

"That's because it doesn't exist," Alex said. "It is a metal that, according to ancient texts, was mined in Atlantis."

"Well, Madoc believed it was real, and so did his father, the king. Madoc returned to North America at the head of a fleet of ten ships, intent on exploring and establishing a colony. They were never heard from again, but people across the Midwest have found what they claim are markers left behind by Madoc and his followers as they journeyed across America. Legend holds that they settled somewhere in the Pacific Northwest. Hunters and trappers in the region would report encounters with light-skinned natives, many with blue or green eyes, whose language included a handful of Welsh words."

"I take it Lewis and Clark didn't find them," Alex said dryly.

"Or maybe they did, and that's why Meriwether Lewis was murdered."

"But he committed suicide," Constance said.

"He was shot in the chest and then the head. Doesn't sound like any suicide I've ever heard of."

"What would be the motive?" Constance asked.

"Lewis was on his way to meet Thomas Jefferson when he died. Maybe he was ready to spill whatever secret he'd been keeping, and somebody couldn't let that happen."

"Like who?" Alex asked.

"Some say the Illuminati helped Jefferson get elected. He was thinking about breaking ranks with them, but the murder of Lewis was enough to shut him up. Same reason he never acknowledged his colored family, but that's another story."

"What would Lewis and Clark have found out here that the Illuminati would kill to cover up?" Alex asked.

"Lower your voice," Constance hissed. "The lumberjacks are staring again."

"I've said too much," Milton said. "Thank you for the drink."

Constance reached out and grabbed Milton's sleeve as he rose from his chair. "Do you have any idea where Trinity went?"

"She might have gone to talk with Harold Moss. I told her to ask him about Ape Canyon." With that, he hurried out the door.

"Well," Alex said. "This gets stranger and stranger."

18- TRACKS IN THE FOREST

Stone turned and strode out of the camp. He took his time, meeting every eye that turned his way. He fixed each man with a serene yet determined stare he'd refined over the years. No one met his eye for long.

"What's our next move?" Moses asked.

"I'm not sure," Stone said. "I want to do some scouting around. You head on back to the truck, let them believe we've blown the joint. I'll meet you there in bit."

Moses seemed to know there would be no point in arguing. "See you in a bit, then," he said. He turned and headed down the well-worn track that led to the dirt road.

Stone waited until his friend was out of sight before getting started. He took time to focus, to drink in the surroundings. The sights, sounds, and smells of the forest drew into sharp focus. He imagined Trinity walking along this same path. What had she been thinking, walking alone into this camp? What had become of her? There were too many possibilities to sort through, nearly all of them unsavory. The one thing he knew for certain was that she had been inside the lumber camp, so that was where he intended to begin. Stealing a glance over his shoulder to make sure no one followed, he stepped off the dirt road and melted into the forest.

Stone was an experienced woodsman. He'd learned

woodscraft as a youth growing up in Virginia, refined it in the service, and continued to master it during the years since. He found it easy to move in silence upon the soft earth here, and the trees provided more than adequate cover. He crept unseen back to the lumber camp and watched.

It wasn't long before Davis turned up. The man wore a sour expression, and paced back and forth, head down, hands in pockets. The lumberjacks filtered out of the camp and back to work until only Davis and another man remained. Stone crept closer as the two began to speak.

"…have a feeling we haven't seen the last of that fellow," the second man was saying.

"Nothing I can do about that. And we don't have anything to hide. The woman came here, asked a few questions, and then she left."

"I know that, and you know that, but he doesn't seem the sort to be so easily convinced."

Stone breathed a sigh of relief. Trinity hadn't been taken or harmed by the men in the lumber camp. That had seemed the simplest and likeliest scenario. But if she wasn't here, then what had happened to her?

He sat listening for a short while, but the men's conversation turned to business. No further mention of Trinity. Satisfied, Stone resumed his search.

Stone worked his way in a slowly expanding circle around the camp, keeping an eye open for signs that Trinity had passed this way. He knew it was possible that she had simply taken the road back to town, in which case her footprints would likely be obscured by the feet that had trodden and vehicles that had driven the route. But he knew Trinity, knew her persistence and downright stubbornness. He was certain she would not have left the camp without nosing around a bit first.

He grinned. That was something the two of them apparently had in common.

He searched until the sounds of the camp grew distant. How much longer should he continue before giving it up and going to meet Moses? Somehow, he couldn't shake the feeling that there was something here to find. He would give it a bit longer.

He stepped into a patch of deep shade and a feeling of foreboding washed over him. Here the massive trees grew close together, denying the sun's light and warmth. He halted, closed his eyes, and allowed himself to feel his surroundings. He knew in an instant that it was more than just deep shade. Something was...wrong about this place.

He took a deep breath through his nostrils. He caught the faint scent of something wild, primitive. He couldn't quite place it, but it sent a shiver down his spine. Whatever it was, he hoped Trinity had not run across it.

Something caught his eye and he knelt for a closer inspection. A partial print, the heel of a small boot. His heart raced. He could not say for certain that it belonged to Trinity, but it certainly could be. And he doubted any man in the lumber camp wore such a small shoe. He scanned the surrounding area and found a few more prints, shallow and faint. They vanished after a few paces.

Stone began a careful inspection of the surrounding area. There had to be something here. Tracking was difficult with so many pine needles lining the forest floor, but he finally found another print deeper in the forest, then another. Trinity, he was now certain it was her, had definitely been moving away from the road, and not in the direction of the camp. So where had she been going?

He kept moving in that direction, picking up an

occasional sign—a broken twig, a scuff at the base of a tree. And then a larger print caught his eye. A large work boot, like the ones worn by the camp workers, headed in the same direction as the smaller prints. Had Trinity been chased, or perhaps stalked?

He was determined not to give in to the worst case scenario. It was possible that Trinity had merely been snooping around and someone had followed to see what she was up to. The presence of another person did not necessarily mean that she had met with foul play.

He continued his search, but the footprints disappeared. He searched all around, but could spot no more signs. It was as if both people had up and vanished. Of course, that was absurd. There were plenty of reasons that they would leave no obvious tracks as they moved deeper into the forest, the dense layer of leaves being foremost among them.

He kept up the search for another half an hour just to be certain, but he finally had to give it up. He would learn no more from tracking them.

And then he saw it.

Clear as day, in the middle of a patch of exposed earth, a massive footprint. He moved in for a closer look, being careful not to disturb it.

The length was a good eighteen inches, perhaps longer, and about ten inches wide. The toes were long, with an oversized big toe. A few feet farther along, he saw another partial print.

"Well now," Stone said, "what sort of beast left these tracks?"

Before he could give them a closer inspection, a large figure charged out of the forest and made a beeline for Stone. He rolled to the side as a stout wooden club buried itself in the earth where he had knelt seconds before. He sprang to his feet only to be confronted by another big man, this one wielding an axe. The man swung the weapon at Stone's head. Stone ducked and the blade missed him by inches. He struck the man with a stiff right cross, sending him staggering back.

Stone whirled around just in time to see the first attacker coming at him again. He dodged another blow of the club, then struck back with two sharp punches that opened the man's nose. The fellow backed away a few steps, club raised. Over his shoulder, Stone saw the axe man moving in. The two had him hemmed in.

"I would hate to use deadly force here," Stone said. "Why don't the two of you tell me what your problem is and we'll see what we can work out."

"You are poking around where you don't belong," the man with the club said.

"I'm just looking for my friend," Stone replied.

"Liar. You're from the government."

"What would the government want with a lumber camp?" Stone asked, slowly moving his hand toward the spot where he carried his Webley concealed beneath his loose fitted shirt. It wasn't ideal for quick access.

"It's not the lumber camp, idiot," axe man said in a German accent.

"Shut your mouth, Ernst," barked the club wielder, who was now holding his weapon up like a baseball bat.

"What does it matter? I am about to kill him."

Stone sensed rather than saw Ernst move. He reached for his weapon, but before Ernst had taken two steps, something struck him from behind. He fell flat on his face, revealing Moses standing behind him.

"Had a feeling you could use some help," Moses said.

"You were right."

The man with the club gaped, then turned and ran. Stone sprinted after him. Perhaps Trinity had stumbled across whatever secret these men were trying to protect. If so, he might know something about what happened to her.

It was growing dark, and the dense forest made it impossible to see more than a few feet ahead. Stone and Moses followed the sound of the fleeing man. Their boots slipped on the thick carpet of pine needles that made tracking impossible. The ground sloped sharply downward, and they half ran, half slid forward.

A bloodcurdling shriek split the air. It continued on, slowly fading away. Stone winced. He had heard a man cry out like that only once in his life, in Tibet when a climber had fallen off a ledge. The drop had been a thousand feet and it had seemed like an eternity before the man's cries no longer echoed in his ears.

They came to a cliff, partially hidden by low fir trees. A box canyon lay below them. It was a precipitous drop down to a forest so thick that you could not see the ground.

"I don't think he survived," Moses said dryly. "Sorry about that."

They searched around but they could find no tracks that would tell them where the men had come from. Finally, they returned to the spot where Stone had discovered the large tracks.

Moses tensed when he saw it. "You know how I feel about the supernatural."

"Relax. If these Bigfoot exist, they're living creatures like any other. Wild animals don't scare you, do they?"

Moses folded his powerful arms and fixed Stone with

a knowing smile. "You telling me if a bunch of gorillas came trooping out of the forest, you wouldn't be scared?"

"I have encountered gorillas in the wild and yes, I had a healthy respect for them. But they behaved like any other intelligent, social creature. Leave them alone and they'll leave you alone. And these things are supposed to have intelligence much closer to that of humans."

"And would you say humans are more or less prone to senseless violence than gorillas?" Moses asked.

"Point taken," Stone said. "But it's a moot point. This track is a fake."

"You sure?" Moses relaxed a little bit, but was still giving the print a wide berth.

"It's too flat. If this were an actual pint, certain parts of the foot like the big toe and ball of the foot would sink deeper into the earth. You step and push off, making a deeper indentation with the front of the foot." He flattened his palm, pressed it to the ground, and made a rolling motion to illustrate.

"I'm not a tenderfoot," Moses said.

"You're acting like one. Here, take a look and see for yourself."

Moses glared at him, clenched his fists, and came to stand beside his friend. As soon as his eyes fell on the large print, he smiled.

"Looks to me like some joker cut out wooden feet and strapped them to their boots. It don't look natural."

Stone nodded approvingly. "Go on. What else?"

Emboldened, Moses knelt beside the partial print a few feet away. "The length of the stride is all wrong, too. A man can put on a pair of big feet, but he can't make his legs two feet longer. Look how close together these are."

"I'm glad we see it the same," Stone said. "The

question is, why would someone plant fake Bigfoot prints out here in the forest?"

INTERLUDE 5

May, 1927
Five Years Ago

Stone came to with cold water splashing on his face. His eyes still burned. He sat up and looked around, but he could not see. He was still blind.

"What have you done to me?"

"There is nothing wrong with your eyes." Gideon's voice seemed to fill the space around him.

"Why can't I see?"

"You must be born again. Like a child in the womb. You are sightless now, but you will see again. If you survive your birth."

Stone touched his eyes, blinked. He wished he could know for certain that he still had his eyesight. He reached out and his hand found a smooth, cold stone wall. He stood and felt his way along the wall, trying to take the measure of the space in which he was confined.

"What do you mean by 'survive the birth'?" He asked.

"Childbirth is painful and traumatic."

"That doesn't bode well for me."

"I assure you the process is infinitely more painful for the one who is birthing the child."

"That doesn't make me feel any better." Stone turned a corner, felt his way along the next wall.

"It was not intended for comfort. It is simply the truth," Gideon said.

Stone completed a circuit of the room. He was in a cell

about twenty feet square. A metal door without a knob or hinges was set in one wall. He explored the edges with the tips of his fingers, pushed and tugged, but it would not budge. With a growl of frustration, he threw his shoulder into the door. Sharp, stabbing pain was his lone reward.

Something struck him across the shins. He let out a grunt of pain and threw a wild punch that struck only open air. In a flash, his feet were swept out from under him, and he landed hard on the stone floor. Before he could regain his feet, something struck him across the base of the skull and he slumped to the ground, dazed.

A rain of sharp blows poured down upon him. He tried to fight back, but his punches and kicks were useless against his unseen assailant, who moved on silent feet in the darkness.

Without warning, the attack ended. Stone lurched to his feet, excruciating scorching every inch of his flesh. He tried in vain to get his hands on his attacker, but the person was gone.

He was alone in the darkness.

19- APE CANYON

Harold Moss lived in a cabin in the general vicinity of the lumber camp Stone and Moses had visited the evening before. Stone, Constance, and Alex paid him a visit. Moses had been tasked with paying a visit to the general store to see if either of the shopkeepers could shed any light on the Lewis and Clark legends.

Harold Moss was a wizened old man with a full head of flyaway hair like white candy floss and a beard that would have made Rip Van Winkle proud. He seemed surprised but pleased to have visitors. He settled into a handmade rocking chair on the front porch, while the others found seats where they could.

"Ape Canyon, you say? Why would you even ask about something like that?"

"I'm writing a book," Constance said. "People enjoy these sorts of stories."

They had decided to be circumspect about the reason for their visit. If Trinity had met with foul play, there was no telling who might be an enemy.

"I'm not interested in being laughed at." Moss cleared his throat and spat a stream of phlegm-clotted tobacco juice onto the ground.

"Not at all," Constance assured. "All the stories I'm collecting will be presented without judgment. I'm even publishing a graveyard story told to me by my own grandfather."

Moss gazed out at the wall of green that encircled his home. Finally, he nodded.

"It happened back in 1924. That was the year Calvin Coolidge did his inaugural address over the radio. Never thought I'd hear one of those with my own ears. Anyhow, we were working a gold claim, me and a few other fellows. My body couldn't handle the digging anymore, so I did most of the panning. We had been working there for a few weeks and things were getting strange."

"Strange how?" Constance scribbled notes on a small pad, keeping up the author ruse.

Moss pursed his lips. "Little things at first. Cries in the night. Big things moving in the darkness so fast and silent it was like they could float over the ground."

"What did the cries sound like?" Constance asked.

Moss tugged thoughtfully at his beard. "Imagine a fellow with a deep voice trying to imitate a coyote's yipping. It wasn't exactly like that, but that's the best I can come up with. And then there was the drumming."

"Drumming?" Stone frowned. "Are you sure they weren't Indians?"

Moss shook his head. "Not that kind of drumming. More like sticks being banged together. Sometimes big rocks. Sometimes it almost sounded like Morse code to me. Everybody else said I was crazy." He shook his head, his gaze drifting, as if to some faraway place.

"Could it have been natives trying to drive you away from the canyon?"

"Indians won't go near that place. We should have known not to go there." Moss spat again. "One morning, we found a bunch of gear strewn about, some of it smashed. I'm talking pick handles snapped. Wood this thick." He held up his arm, tapped his wrist. "Indians didn't do that. And there were footprints everywhere."

Stone had a feeling he knew what sorts of footprints

the man was talking about.

"Giant bare feet, not quite human. We didn't know what to make of them."

"Were they apelike?" Constance asked.

The man shrugged. "What did any of us know about such things? I don't believe I've ever seen an ape footprint. In any case, a couple fellas wanted to get the hell out of there, but the rest of us wanted to stay. They reckoned that whatever the things were, they were only a nuisance." He paused, took a deep breath. "They didn't consider the possibility that maybe the beasts were giving us fair warning."

Stone leaned forward a little, eager to hear the man's story. Alex and Constance did the same. Moss sat there in silence for so long that Stone began to wonder if the fellow had changed his mind about telling his tale. But finally, the man cleared his throat.

"Things were all right for a few days, until Coleman shot one of them."

Stone sat bolt upright. "Shot one? You mean, you all saw it?"

Moss shook his head. "No. Coleman was hunting alone when he said one of them just burst out of the forest, coming right at him. He had his rifle at the ready, and he fired out of instinct. Said he was fairly certain he only caught it on the hip."

"I'll bet it didn't like that very much." Alex scratched his thigh with his hook, perhaps remembering the serious injury he'd suffered not too long ago.

"None of them like it very much. The injured beast fled. We found blood and a few hairs. We didn't follow it too far. Coleman felt terrible about it. Said if he'd taken even a moment to think about it, he'd have tried to back away, fire into the air, anything but shooting the creature unless it forced him to."

Stone nodded in agreement.

"Anyhow, he couldn't exactly write a letter of apology, and the apes, or whatever they are, turned out to be the unforgiving type."

"What do you mean?" Constance asked.

"That night, they attacked our camp." Moss looked at them, a touch of challenge in his gaze as if daring them to contradict him. When they kept their silence, he continued. "It started out with the usual howling, and drumming, but this time it came from all around, at least twenty, maybe more. It got louder and louder, the beasts coming closer, and then the attack started. Stones were flying, huge things, bigger than grapefruits." He clenched his fists and pressed them together to illustrate. "We hunkered down in the log cabin we'd built and waited."

"How long did it last?" Stone asked.

"Al night. Stones rained down on the roof, cracked it in places. Then they got braver, charged the cabin, and banged on the walls. The whole thing shook like it was being hit by a battering ram. The chinking between the logs started to crumble, and pretty soon gaps opened between the logs and we caught a few glimpses of the creatures."

"What did you see?" Stone found himself intrigued by the old miner's tale.

"Fur, mostly. Or hair—dark, thick, glossy. Not quite like human hair, but not fur, either. Glimpses of bared teeth, eyes…never got a good look at them. Didn't want to get close enough to the wall to peer out." The old man shuddered at the memory. Whatever he had seen and experienced, it had shaken him badly.

"Finally, one of them stuck its arm through. I picked up a chunk of firewood and whacked it. It let out a snarl that just about turned my shorts brown, if you know what I mean. Another fellow slashed it with his knife and it pulled its arm back out. I was afraid that was just going to make them angrier, but they stopped trying to get in after that. They kept up the yowling and throwing rocks, but eventually, they went away."

"What did you do after that?" Constance asked.

"We interpreted the attack as our final warning. Went home and never went back."

"Mister Moss," Constance began, "we've heard tales that the creatures have kidnapped women. Should I be worried?" She let out a nervous laugh.

Moss considered the question, tugging thoughtfully at his beard. Finally, he let out a long, slow breath.

"I'd like to tell you that you have nothing to worry about, but the truth is, I don't know."

"Could you tell us how to get to Ape Canyon?" Constance asked.

"No. I don't remember exactly where it is."

"It wasn't that long ago," Stone reminded him.

"I remember that it's way over on the other side of Mount Saint Helens. I didn't do the driving, and I didn't lead the way going in or out."

"Have you ever tried to find it again?" Stone asked.

"I don't want to go back. A girl came by here a few days back, asking me to show it to her on a map. I tried to help her, but I was stumped. Maybe I don't want to remember."

Stone had been watching Moss carefully. He was highly adept at detecting signs of deception. Moss was telling the truth, as he saw it, about what happened at Ape Canyon, but he was lying about not remembering the location, and Stone sensed Moss was hiding even more.

Constance turned the conversation in a more general direction, asking about the history of Bigfoot sightings in the area. With the topic of Ape Canyon apparently behind them, Moss relaxed visibly and became more expansive with his answers.

When the conversation drew to a close, they thanked the old man for his help and made their way back to the truck, which was parked just out of sight of the cabin. Stone didn't get inside.

"Drive down the road a mile or so and wait for me. I want to keep an eye on the cabin. I think Moss is up to something."

20- UP A TREE

Stone moved into the cover of the trees and circled around until he had a clear view of Moss's cabin. The old man sat on the front porch, but he was no longer rocking in his chair. He leaned forward, hands folded, posture tense. He gazed intently in the direction Stone and his friends had gone.

Finally, the roar of an engine rose above the birdsong as Alex fired up the truck and drove away. Moss visibly relaxed. Moss sat, head craned, listening until the sound of the vehicle faded away. He waited another minute, then stood, descended from the porch, and rounded the cabin.

Stone's heart raced. Moving silently like a predator stalking its prey, he shadowed Moss and the man left the clearing where his cabin stood and plunged into the depths of the forest.

He followed along for a mile or so, Moss continuing in a straight path as if making a beeline for a specific destination. Finally, he slowed. Stone ducked down and crept closer. Suddenly, Moss turned and stared directly at him. Stone froze. He was certain the man had neither heard nor seen him, but Moss seemed to be staring at something. Finally, he gave a single nod and plunged into a dense stand of low-growing trees.

Wary of a trap, Stone rounded the thicket and worked his way back in, intending to pick up the old man's trail. He found it with ease, though Moss's tracks were faint, almost imperceptible. The man moved well in the forest. Stone followed along for a hundred yards as the way suddenly grew steep. The footprints vanished in a narrow, rocky wash where rainwater and snowmelt had eroded the soil. He paused, listening for the sound of movement. Moss couldn't be too far ahead of him, and Stone's hearing, sharpened by training in Tibet, was unmatched. He heard nothing. The man must have gone to ground somewhere up ahead.

Stone considered the situation. He had nothing to fear from the old man, but he wanted to find out what the fellow was up to, and he couldn't do that if Moss thought Stone was following him. In fact, Stone might have already blown it. If Moss were aware of his presence and was hiding from him, Stone could either confront him and demand answers or try and wait him out. But in the first case, Moss would probably head back to his cabin. Stone would try to wait him out.

He selected a tree that appeared primed for climbing. He'd ascend it until he had a clear view of the surrounding area, then wait for Moss to show himself. He'd catch up with Alex and Trinity later. The pair would realize he wasn't coming back right away and would head back to town.

He chose a sturdy-looking limb, leaped, and grabbed hold. He swung himself up with the grace of a gymnast. He'd done more than his share of climbing in just about every environment and scenario imaginable. He ascended quickly, and soon found himself a good thirty feet off the ground. He dared not go any higher, lest the branches not support his weight.

Even at this short distance off the ground, the air was less dank. A light breeze ruffled his hair. This would not be a bad place to sit and rest. He hoped it wouldn't be long, though.

He heard a soft sound in the distance. Someone was trying to move quietly. Oddly, the noise came from the direction of the cabin. Had Moss managed to slip past him? He turned in the direction of the noise and scanned the area. He saw bits of color. Someone was hiding, imperfectly, behind a tree.

"You might as well come out," he said.

An attractive woman stepped out into the open. Her light brown skin, glossy black hair, and high cheekbones hinted at native ancestry, but her nose and eyes suggested mixed race. She folded her arms and glared up at him. She was clad in a man's shirt and dungarees, but it did nothing to hide her feminine charms.

"I have to say, you're the biggest bird I've ever seen."

Stone flashed a grin and clambered down. She met him at the base of the tree.

"You're good. Most people can't hear me coming."

Stone shrugged. "I have good hearing."

"You got a name?" the woman asked.

"Yes. Do you?"

She tapped her foot impatiently. "You're on our land, and you're the gentleman. So that's two reasons for you to introduce yourself first."

"I'm Brock Stone."

"I'm Marian Moss," she said simply. "Now, why are you stalking my father?"

"Your father?" Stone couldn't mask his surprise. Marian couldn't have been older than her late twenties. Then again, it wasn't exactly unheard of for someone to father a child later in life. He couldn't but wonder what Marian's mother had looked like. She certainly didn't get her looks from Moss.

"Harold Moss," she said simply.

"Yes, I just had a talk with him. He's an interesting fellow."

Marian arched an eyebrow. "Interesting enough that you decided to skulk around on our place?"

Stone trusted his instincts, and right now they were telling him to be truthful with this woman.

"I'm looking for a friend, a woman, who disappeared in these parts not too long ago. I know she met with your father."

"Are you accusing my father of being a kidnapper?" She took a step closer to him. "Because if you are, I'll thank you to get off of our land right now."

Stone doubted Moss owned much, if any, of the forest that surrounded his cabin, but didn't think that point was worth arguing at the moment.

"No, not at all." He paused. "I know it sounds ridiculous, but I keep hearing there are creatures around here who have been known to kidnap women."

"Bigfoot, you mean. I'm disappointed in you, Mister Stone. You don't seem the sort to believe in fairy tales."

"Let's just say I've seen enough of the world that I no longer dismiss the implausible as being impossible. Besides, your father says he knows for a fact that they're real."

Marian shook her head. "He's old, confused. Besides, that doesn't explain why you're wandering around out here."

"I sensed your father wasn't entirely forthcoming with me. I waited, and sure enough, he waited a couple minutes and then made a beeline for this area. He's holed up somewhere around here."

"I doubt that. He's better in the woods than I am, and it seems he's better than you, too."

"Fair enough. I'll just search around on my own until I find whatever it is he's hiding." He held up a hand. "And don't try to divert me with claims that this is your land. I'm certain you don't own the entire forest. Even if you did, good luck stopping me."

"What do you believe you are going to find?" Her voice was dull, sullen.

"Ape Canyon?" Stone guessed. "Your father said my friend was looking for it. He claims it's somewhere on the other side of the mountain, but I think it's much closer."

Marian stood, arms folded, brown eyes staring daggers at him. Then her shoulders sagged and her gaze softened.

"Fine. I'll show you the way, but those creatures never kidnapped anybody."

21- THE SECRET

Stone followed Marian up a steep incline, moving in the general direction that Moss had gone several minutes earlier. He found himself on high alert, wondering if she might be leading him into some sort of trap. His gut told him otherwise, but it was best to remain vigilant.

Off to his right, he spotted a few signs of Moss's trail—partial footprints, a broken twig. The fellow had grown careless. Perhaps he'd seen Marian approach Stone and seized upon the opportunity to get out of there. In any case, the tracks led back toward the cabin, which was fine with him.

Marian saw him looking. "He's gone. He'll be angry that I showed you this, but it's better than having you poking around back here where you're not wanted."

Stone didn't reply. He didn't much care what the woman thought of him as long as she either provided him with a clue to find Trinity or helped him mark her father off of his list of suspects.

A gentle breeze carried with it a whiff of something feral, like a polecat or a fox's den. Stone crinkled his nose.

"It's just up here." Marian pointed to a cave, its entrance almost entirely obscured by fallen rocks.

"What's inside?"

"Just follow me." She led the way into the cave, the air inside cool, but oddly fresh.

They worked their way down a series of slippery declines and loose rock piles, the faint glow from the cave mouth lighting their way, until they came to a dead end.

Or so Stone thought.

"You might have trouble squeezing through here." Marian pointed to a narrow passageway hidden in shadow.

Stone could see well in the dark, but he'd overlook it. As predicted, he had a difficult time forcing his muscular body through the opening, but he managed to squeeze through until the going became a bit easier. He was still forced to turn sideways, but at least he could breathe. The passage made a sharp bend, and up ahead he could see a sliver of light.

"Another squeeze, I'm afraid." Marian slipped through, blotting out the light for a moment, and then Stone followed.

He found himself standing on a ledge overlooking a tiny box canyon. Trees ringed the rim, obscuring the view from above and casting long shadows on the forest below. One could fly right over it and probably not take notice. A few feet below where they stood, a natural spring poured a gentle stream of clear water down to the canyon below.

"Is this Ape Canyon?" he asked.

Marian made a noncommittal gesture. "It connects to the canyon where my father was attacked by a narrow passageway. It's one of the few ways in and out."

"So, what is special about this place?"

"They live down there."

Stone did a double-take. "The Bigfoot?"

"A small troop of them. They're only around in warm weather. We think they migrate south in the winter, probably all the way down to California."

Stone blinked a few times, taking in what Marian was saying. "Do they interact with you?"

"Not directly, but every once in a while one will let

itself be seen. They also vocalize when we leave food for them. Saying thank you, I guess."

"What do they eat?"

"Judging by their scats, they're omnivores just like us. We give them vitamin-rich fruits, leafy greens, things that will help balance their diet."

Stone blinked a few times, taking in what Marian was saying. Bigfoot was real!

Stone nodded. In the early days of seafaring, sailors had suffered from scurvy and other health problems due to a lack of essential vitamins and minerals their limited diet did not provide. Even soldiers in the field had similar complaints. Ship captains and military officers had taken to providing citrus fruits and cider to balance out the diets of those in their charge.

Stone scanned the valley below, his sharp eyes picking out minute details within the mass of green. A bird perched on a limb, a squirrel scrambled up a tree trunk. But no sign of a giant furry beast.

"Why is your father doing this? He was nearly killed by these things."

"He believes the Bigfoot could have killed the miners if they wanted to, but instead they gave the men one last chance to escape."

"Even though a miner shot one of their own," Stone added.

"Exactly. He thinks they are worth caring for."

"So, your father is their...protector?"

"I think that's what he considers himself, although they probably don't need his help. They can look out for themselves just fine." Marian's flinty gaze softened as she stared down into the valley. "He's worried that the logging industry will grow to the point that the creatures are driven away as their habitat shrinks."

Stone considered this. It probably would happen, eventually, considering how many Americans were moving west in search of new opportunities, but this land was so vast and untouched that it would take centuries for that to happen. And then he remembered something that Davis, the logging foreman, had said.

"Has your father been messing with things at the logging site?"

Marian hesitated, then nodded. "I'm certain he has, though he's never admitted it. He once told me that someone ought to spike every tree in the Pacific Northwest just to make it more difficult for the loggers." She sighed. "I know that makes him sound like a bad man, but his intentions are good. He only wants to look out for the creatures."

"Was it he who left fake Bigfoot tracks near the mining camp?"

"Not a chance. He wouldn't want to leave any evidence that these creatures are real, much less that they live around here."

"Are they down there right now?" Stone asked, his eyes still searching, probing.

"You never know. They range widely and can move like shadows in the forest."

"And you don't believe the stories of these creatures kidnapping women?" Stone asked sharply, trying to catch her off guard.

"No. All they want is to be left alone. They always keep their distance from humans unless they feel they are in danger. I've been close to them a few times and none of them have ever made a move toward me."

Stone nodded. He hadn't considered it likely that these

Bigfoot creatures had taken Trinity. But why was she looking for them at all?

"And you aren't pulling my leg?" he asked.

"Of course I'm not lying. What did you think you would find out here if not Bigfoot?"

"I was looking for Trinity, not Bigfoot. If you have any idea what happened to her, please tell me."

Marian lowered her head. "I don't know what happened to her, and that's the God's honest truth."

"I know where she went." They turned to see Harold Moss approaching. A pained expression painted his face, and he didn't quite meet Stone's eye. "I'm afraid something has happened to that girl and it's all my fault."

Alex hadn't driven more than a quarter of a mile before Constance ordered him to stop. There was a note of command to her voice that caught Alex so completely by surprise that instinctively slammed on the brakes. The Roadster skidded to a halt on the mountain road, kicking up a cloud of dust and gravel.

"What's wrong?" he asked.

Constance ignored him. She reached underneath her seat and pulled out a rucksack.

"What's in there?"

"Turn your head," she snapped as she pulled a pair of dungarees from the bag. Her sharp tone and the hard look in her eyes, made her seem like a different person.

"You can't wait until we get back to town before changing clothes?" He felt his cheeks warm at the sound of rustling clothing.

"No," she said simply.

A few seconds later he heard the passenger door open. He turned to see Constance, now dressed in pants, shirt, and boots, slide out of the cab.

"Where are you going?" he asked.

"There's no time to explain." Constance hurried around to the driver's side and spoke to him through the window. "I'm trained to read people. Moss was lying. Every time the subject of the Bigfoot or Ape Canyon came up, his eyes flitted in the same direction. I'm going to catch up with Stone. He might need help."

"You?" Alex scratched his head with the tip of his hook. "I should come with you."

"That's gallant of you, but you would slow me down. Go get Moses. I will leave a trail in the forest for you to follow. Look for broken branches pointing the way."

Alex blinked, surprise rendering him mute. This was not the Constance he thought he knew.

"I owe you an explanation," she said, "but there's no time." She climbed up onto the running board and planted a kiss on his lips. "I promise I'll tell you everything. Just trust me."

With that, she hopped nimbly to the ground, turned, and sprinted into the forest. In a matter of seconds, she was gone.

INTERLUDE 6

May, 1927
Five Years Ago

Stone awoke to the aroma of freshly baked bread. He felt around and found a slice of warm bread with butter and a few tart berries, Himalayan blackberries perhaps. There was also a cup of water and a cup of hot tea. He devoured it all, even the tea, which he ordinarily did not care for.

"Did you enjoy your meal?" Gideon's voice asked from somewhere in the darkness.

"I would love a cup of coffee," Stone said wryly.

"I just like the smell of coffee. I could smell it on your breath the first time we met."

"It has been days since I had coffee. You must have a sensitive nose."

"Or you have bad breath."

Stone breathed into his cupped hands, sniffed, and shrugged. He stood and stretched. Every inch of his body hurt. He wondered what was in store for him today.

"What comes next?" Stone asked.

"Your rebirth continues," Gideon said.

"You said childbirth is painful, so I guess that means another beating?"

"That depends on you."

Stone was tired, hurting, and had little patience for the man's cryptic answers.

"Can we get on with it then?"

"First lesson," Gideon said. "Inside the womb, a child who is nearing birth cannot see the world outside, but that doesn't mean the child is unaware.

"Makes sense," Stone said.

"Tell me what you hear."

"Your voice," Stone replied. He waited. Silence. "Sorry. Was I supposed to listen for something else?"

Something struck him across the small o his back. A lance of pain burned his flesh.

"Ouch. I only wanted a clarification of the rules."

This time the blow struck him across the knees. He let out a pained grunt.

"An infant is incapable of understanding rules. It learns by experience." Still, Gideon's voice seemed to come from everywhere at once.

"How do you do that with your voice?"

Something jabbed him hard in the gut. Stone grunted.

"Focus!" Gideon snapped.

"All right. I'm focusing. Let's try it again."

Gideon didn't reply. The silence was as complete as the darkness.

Stone listened for more sounds. He had sharp ears, but he couldn't hear anything except the thrum of his heartbeat. A whack across his backside, more annoying than painful, made him jump.

"I can hear my heartbeat."

That must have been a satisfactory answer because Gideon didn't hit him this time.

"What else?" Gideon said.

"There's a rushing sound in my ears like the blowing wind."

"And outside of yourself?"

Try as he would, Stone couldn't hear anything.

Another blow. He tried to shut out his other senses and focus on his hearing. He tuned out the scent of blood that filled his nostrils, the taste of sweat on his tongue.

"Wait a minute." He heard a faint dripping sound. "There's water dripping somewhere far away."

"Find it."

It took a long time to find the source of the sound, and Gideon hit him with the stick several times before he completed the task, but he managed it. There was a crack in the wall several feet up. He pressed his ear to the small opening. The water was dripping on the other side of the wall.

"I found it."

Silence.

He waited. NO answer. "Are you still there?"

No answer.

"No prize for passing your test?" he muttered. "Not even a pat on the head?"

As if in response, there was a scraping sound somewhere behind him. A familiar aroma, rich and nutty, filled the air. He smiled, followed the scent like a bloodhound. His hands closed around a cup of lukewarm coffee. He took a sip and let out a sigh of contentment.

"Thank you," he said.

From somewhere far away, Gideon replied.

"You are welcome."

22- INTO THE CANYON

Stone scaled the cliff with spiderlike agility, finding handholds and footholds that most climbers would never spot. He was moving rapidly, almost recklessly, but if Trinity were in danger, he didn't want to waste a precious second.

"Please, let her be alive," he whispered aloud.

No, he couldn't think like that. She was all right. She had to be.

Upon learning where Trinity had gone, he had asked Harold and Marian to bring his friends up to speed when they returned. They would be unhappy that he had left them behind, but hopefully would understand.

The sheer cliff ended at a boulder field choked with shrubs and stunted trees. It sloped down a hundred yards to a forest-covered canyon floor.

Something moved at the corner of Stone's eye. A flash of brown and no more. He tensed. Had it been a Bigfoot, or something more commonplace, like a bear? And then the wind changed directions and he caught a whiff of something unpleasant, like the smell of a wet dog. That was no bear.

He circled the boulder field, keeping to the shelter of the forest. He moved quickly and silently, closing in on the spot where he had seen something moving. When he arrived there, he searched the forest floor until he spotted a small indentation in the needle-covered floor. It might be a toeprint. It would take something very heavy to leave even that much of an indentation.

He headed in the direction he believed the creature had gone, searching for spoor. He had gone only about fifty yards when he came to a spot where the low-hanging limbs had been snapped off of the tree trunks up to a height of about ten feet. Some of these limbs had been as thick as Stone's forearm, and the breaks were clean. The strength required to do it would have to be tremendous. The pattern of broken limbs continued on, creating a pathway through the dense jungle.

"Just right for a very tall beast to walk upright without bumping its head," Stone muttered.

Stone ducked into the forest and moved parallel to the path until it came to an end at a spring-fed pool of water at the base of a cliff. Again he caught a pungent, animal odor, much stronger this time.

Like a bloodhound, he followed his nose. He crept through the forest until he spotted a clearing up ahead. He froze.

A huge, hairy ape man was striding purposefully toward the canyon wall. The creature stood eight feet tall. Its shoulders, back, and thighs were thick with muscle that rippled as it walked. Its arms were very long compared to its human cousins, the fingertips almost reaching its knees. And the thing was covered from head to toe with glossy, reddish-brown fur.

Stone couldn't deny it. Bigfoot was real.

He watched as the creature scaled the canyon wall up to a rock overhang. Stone caught a glimpse of another creature, a juvenile, peering over the ledge.

That must be where their den is, Stone thought.

Now he had a decision to make. It had been Marian's opinion that the Bigfoot had not taken Trinity. But what if she was mistaken? He fixed his eyes on the overhang. To get there he would have to cross an open clearing then climb thirty feet up the canyon wall without being spotted. That was impossible. But could he leave here without trying?

Just then a grapefruit-sized rock whistled through the air like a Walter Johnson fastball and smashed into the ground about ten feet from where Stone knelt. He immediately ducked behind the scant cover of a juniper. One of the beasts had thrown it at him. But had the creature been trying to kill him, or was it a warning?

The forest all around him was suddenly filled with loud clacking sounds, like sticks being knocked together. The sounds were coming closer. And then came the howling. Well, some of the vocalizations sounded like howls, but he also heard yips and guttural roars.

Another rock flew and it struck in the same spot as before. Not a miss, then. The Bigfoot wanted him to leave. Reluctantly he moved in the opposite direction of the clacking and howling, away from the den. He would scour the canyon for signs of Trinity. If he found none, he would return.

The sounds were spreading out now until they had flanked him. Stone realized he was being herded deeper into the slot canyon, away from the Moss family cabin.

Here the dense canopy cast the forest in shadows. Dark shapes appeared in the dim light, coming closer until he could see the beasts clearly. They were huge, seven to nine feet tall with broad shoulders, barrel chests, and thick, overlong arms and legs. Their fur was glossy and ranged from auburn to almost black. Their faces were simian; intelligence brimmed in eyes that were eerily human.

The Bigfoot troop continued to close in, clacking their rocks and sticks, slapping trees, and emitting throaty grunts and growls.

Cold sweat ran down the back of Stone's neck. He took a step back and drew his Webley. He didn't wish to harm these fantastic creatures, but he would defend his own life with deadly force if necessary.

Soft footsteps shuffled nearby. He spun about, searching for the source of the sound. He spotted it immediately.

A gorgeous woman stood in front of him. Her fair skin was bruised and scraped. Her auburn hair was pulled up in a bun. Wonder shone in her big brown eyes.

"Stone? What are you doing here?

23-TRINITY'S STORY

A smile spread across his face. "Trinity! Thank heaven you're alive." For a moment, he forgot all about the Bigfoot. When he looked back, he realized they had all gone silent at Trinity's appearance.

"You don't need that," she said, indicating the Webley with a nod of her head. "They simply want you to move along. This is their part of the canyon. Follow me."

She led him through the narrow crevasse and emerged onto a ledge overlooking another box canyon. This one was deeper than the smaller one from which he had just come. A river wended its way through the forest below.

Stone had no interest in admiring the view. He wrapped his arms around Trinity's waist and pulled her close, trying to convince himself she was real. Trinity draped her arms around his neck and rested her head on his chest.

"I am very happy to see you," she murmured. "But I did not need you to rescue me."

He lowered his head to kiss her and paused, crinkled his nose.

"What's wrong?" she asked.

"I'm sorry, but you usually smell… pleasant."

"I've been down in this canyon for days. Of course I'm

going to smell… earthy."

"If that's what you want to call it." He leaned down and kissed her gently.

Trinity let out a soft whimper and for a split second, she seemed to melt. Suddenly she stiffened and pushed him away.

"What are you doing here? How did you even know where to look for me?" She gave him a playful punch in the chest.

"Your friend Constance came to me for help after she didn't hear from you for a week."

"Constance? I don't have a friend by that name." Trinity pursed her lips and fixed him with a suspicious stare. "Who is this person, exactly?"

"About your age. Blonde, fair skin, a bit on the prim and proper side."

"You mean Connie." Trinity closed her eyes and let out a low groan. "She's not my friend."

"She knows quite a lot about you," Stone said, wondering if he had been duped.

"She's a librarian. I sort of collected her when I started investigating John Kane. She's nice enough, but she's a strange one."

"How so?"

"If she isn't popping by unannounced, she's 'accidentally' bumping into me at various places around the city. I've tried to gently create some distance between us but she's persistent. She's quite bright and is good company, but I think she's lonely and unskilled at making friends."

"Spending too much time with your nose in a book will do that to you. Look at Alex." Stone cocked his head. "Speaking of, he and Constance appear to have taken a shine to one another. Perhaps he can occupy some of her free time." He paused. Trinity's face had twisted into a puzzled frown. "What's the matter?"

"I never told Connie where I was going. Only that I would be gone for a few weeks at the very least."

"She knew you had visited the offices of the *Seattle Spokesman*," Stone said. "Do you think she could be a plant from Kane's organization?"

Trinity appeared troubled. "I suppose it's possible, but my instincts say no. Probably she sweet-talked the information out of my editor. I had to give him enough details to get approval for the trip."

"You gave her a note to give to me," Stone reminded her. "Unfortunately, she had a mishap and ruined it. I could only make out a few words."

"Note?" Trinity frowned. "I didn't write any note."

Stone froze. He was seeing things in a different light. If the note was forged, then maybe Constance's odd decision to travel by canoe was part of the ruse.

"We'll get to the bottom of things when we find her. Come on. Let's get out of here." He put his arm around her but she pulled away.

"We can't go now."

"The Bigfoot," he said. "I'm afraid I riled them up by coming too close to their den."

"That is not the reason. It's my investigation. Stone, you will not believe what I have found in Ape Canyon!"

When Alex walked into the general store, Moses was sipping coffee and bumping gums with Vince and Deb, regaling them with tales from his professional boxing career. A gifted storyteller when the mood struck him, he had the shopkeepers in stitches.

"And I said to the referee, 'Ain't a boxer this side of Gene Tunny can hit that hard. Check his gloves again.' Sure enough, he had switched to gloves with half the padding hollowed out." Moses broke off the story when he saw the expression on Alex's face.

Alex began filling them in on what had transpired. As soon as he mentioned Harold Moss, the blood drained from Deb's face. She glanced at Vince who shook his head.

"Did Moss tell you where Ape Canyon is?" Deb asked.

"Only that it's somewhere on the other side of Mount Saint Helens," Alex said. "Stone didn't believe him and neither did Constance. They both ran off into the forest searching for it."

Deb swore and Vince banged his fist on the counter.

"What's wrong?" Alex asked.

"I was afraid this would happen," Deb said. "Ape Canyon is close by and the Bigfoot is very real. Locals have done our best to hide its location."

"Because of the Bigfoot?"

"That's part of it," she said. "But that's not the main reason." She turned and took a rifle down off the wall. "There's something else going on in that canyon, and your friends are walking right into the middle of it."

At the far end of Ape Canyon, a ramshackle wooden building stood in the shelter of a pine grove. The structure appeared to be on the verge of falling down. The weathered planks that formed the walls were warped and cracked. It appeared as if a stiff breeze would knock it over.

"It looks like a big miner's shack."

"That's what they want you to think," Trinity said.

"What *who* wants me to think?" Stone asked.

"I'm not sure. Either John Kane or the Illuminati. Or maybe Kane is Illuminati. There's no evidence of that, but their symbology keeps cropping up in my work, so I wouldn't be surprised if there is a connection."

"You say that so calmly." Stone couldn't help but admire Trinity's courage. He only wished her bravery didn't get her into so many dangerous situations.

"Why be afraid when I have a gentleman friend who insists on following me across the country because he thinks I need to be rescued?"

Stone didn't know whether to laugh or cry. Only Trinity could get herself caught between Bigfoot and an Illuminati outpost and still believe she did not need help. And perhaps she didn't.

"Those rickety walls are a façade. There's a building inside of it. A block building that has been painted black to camouflage it. I've seen a few men from the mining camp come and go, carrying in supplies. I've been watching this place for days. I've also heard pleas for help, cries of pain, some of them so unearthly I can scarcely believe a human made them."

"Any idea what they're up to?"

"No, but I'm convinced that it is connected with that strange room underneath the Martha Washington School."

"Medical or biological, then," Stone said, scratching his chin thoughtfully. "This has to be an inconvenient location to do that sort of thing."

"Perhaps they want to keep it a secret." Trinity's voice

dripped with sarcasm.

"There are plenty of isolated locations that are much more convenient to Kane's headquarters in New York City. Why go to the opposite coast?"

"That is where the Bigfoot comes in. About ten years ago, Kane started conducting covert research into the Bigfoot. That would be unusual enough, but he was only interested in the mountains of Washington. That led me to his logging business, which has never turned a profit, and a series of unusually high donations to a girls school in Seattle."

"It was the Martha Washington School that brought it all together, wasn't it?" Stone asked. "Kane's money, Ward's connection with the lumber camp, and Junina, the girl from Rockmire who had a Bigfoot sighting so traumatic that it drove her half-mad."

"Look at who just caught up!" Trinity patted him on the arm. "I want to get inside but there's always a guard at the door. That's where you come in."

"Me?"

"Look me in the eye and tell me you can't disable a single guard. That's all they ever post. I don't think they have ever had an uninvited visitor before me. There are only two ways in. One is through the Bigfoot canyon which Moss guards year-round. He doesn't want anyone finding their lair."

"Let me guess. The other way in is guarded by the lumber camp."

Trinity smiled. "I love the way my intelligence has rubbed off on you over the years."

Stone grinned. "I was away for many of those years."

"You don't need to remind me." Trinity grabbed him by the collar and pulled his head down until their noses were almost touching. "Something very bad is going on inside there. We need to find out what. Do it for me. And that's not a request; it's an order." She kissed him firmly on the lips.

"I'll do it, but only because you are such a good kisser," Stone said.

"Why, Brock Stone! What a thing to say!" Trinity said in a mock Southern drawl, fanning air across her face. "I think I might have the vapors."

"I assume you insist on coming along?"

"It's my investigation. You followed *me* here." Any trace of levity was gone. "I have to see it with my own eyes. And we might have to take steps."

24- WARD'S STORY

As they approached the facility, Stone spotted wires running from the structure. His eyes followed them up the trunk of a tall pine. He caught a glimpse of a thick cable running up to a set of shiny discs up in the treetop.

"What are those?" Trinity said.

"I think they might be photovoltaic cells. "They collect power from the sun." Stone said.

"I know the term, and the theory. I didn't think the technology existed."

"Neither did I. You can see it up close and personal once I've dealt with the guard."

"Be careful," Trinity whispered. She punctuated the statement with a kiss on his cheek.

"Always."

Stone crept around the outer wall of the facility. Peering around the corner, he spotted the lone guard. He was an unnaturally large man. His overdeveloped biceps looked like bowling balls stuffed inside his shirt. He sat on a stump, gazing off into the forest. His eyes were barely open, and his posture was one of perfect ease.

Skilled as he was at moving without being seen or heard, Stone only managed to get within twenty feet of the guard before the man cocked his head, sniffed the air, then sprang to his feet.

Stone charged. The guard threw a clumsy punch that Stone ducked. He landed a sharp jab followed by a right cross that broke the big man's nose. The guard threw a powerful left hook that would have caved in Stone's skull had it landed, but this man had chosen to develop his muscles at the expense of quickness and flexibility. Stone dodged the punch and landed a hook of his own to the chin. The guard's eyelids fluttered and his knees wobbled. A side kick to the gut drove the wind out of him and sent him tumbling into a patch of blackberry bushes.

Lips moving silently, eyes afire, the man struggled to get to his feet. His clothing was shredded, every inch of his exposed flesh sliced and scraped by the sharp thorns. He almost managed to get to his feet before Stone's roundhouse kick turned his lights out.

He hastily bound and gagged the guard using the man's own shoelaces and strips of fabric torn from his shredded shirt. He hid the unconscious man within the blackberry patch.

Stone turned to look for Trinity and spotted her opening the door of the facility.

"Wait for me!" he hissed.

She thrust out her lower lip, but waited for him to join her before opening the door.

Inside was a simple room with a concrete floor and block walls. A rickety table and two chairs stood in one corner. A newspaper and a coffee mug sat atop it. To the right, an open door revealed a bedroom with one set of bunks. Clothing lay scattered across the floor.

Farther down on the right was a closed door. Stone pressed his ear to it. A radio was playing a familiar tune—"Between the Devil and the Deep Blue Sea" by Cab Calloway. He heard the clatter of something being dropped on the floor, and then a curse. A moment later, the door began to open.

Stone reached for his Webley. And then he recognized the man on the other side of the door. It was Ward!

Stone grabbed the smaller man by his fleshy throat and forced him back inside the room. Trinity followed and closed the door behind them.

"What is this place?" Stone demanded. He lessened his grip on Ward's throat just enough for the man to speak in a hoarse whisper.

"This is a military facility," Ward gurgled. "You are trespassing on government property."

Stone punched the man in the kidney just hard enough to make Ward's knees buckle and his eyes water. "That is only a taste of the pain I can inflict on you. Don't lie to me again."

"If I were you, I would avoid upsetting him altogether." Trinity spoke in a confidential tone, as if giving advice to a friend.

Ward nodded and took a moment to catch his breath. Finally, he rose on unsteady feet.

"This is a medical facility. We make men bigger and stronger."

"Like that big galoot outside?" Trinity asked.

"He was one of our first patients. We have refined our process a great deal since then."

"Are you making soldiers?" Trinity asked.

"Mercenaries," Stone guessed. "A man like John Kane would sell to the highest bidder."

"That's the way the free market works," Ward said. "But soldiers are only one potential avenue. Workers with tremendous strength and stamina are highly valuable.

And if you make them just bright enough to do the job you need, but not quite intelligent enough to wish for more…" Ward flashed a twisted smile.

"That's not much different from slavery," Trinity said.

Ward had no reply.

"Why this location?" Stone asked.

Ward hesitated but a glare from Stone elicited an answer. "I suppose you could say it was chosen for us. It's a long story."

"Summarize it," Stone said, cracking his knuckles for emphasis.

"Meriwether Lewis discovered this canyon. Jefferson had regaled him with stories of a lost white tribe, so he was shocked to find what appeared to be primitive humans living here. He was fascinated by them and he knew there were those in his party that would hunt the creatures for sport or worse. He also suspected the so-called Corps of Discovery, which made up the backbone of the expedition, was under the sway of the Illuminati."

Stone nodded. The Corps of Discovery was a special unit of the United States Army which had been commissioned by Thomas Jefferson specifically for the Lewis and Clark expedition. The Corps' objectives were to study the plant and animal life and geography of the West and assess its economic potential.

"Was Jefferson an Illuminatus?" Stone asked. Jefferson's political opponents had accused him of not only being connected to the clandestine society, but claimed that he was the head of the American sect of the Illuminati. They had even claimed that, if elected President, he and his fellow intellectuals would strip Americans of their religious freedoms and property rights.

"Not as far as I know. At times, he was forced to be their creature, but he tried to confound them as often as he could. Some of the clues Lewis followed were taken from an artifact discovered in a secret Illuminate temple in Virginia that Jefferson's men raided. A runestone, I believe."

Stone nodded, remembering the temple he and Alex had discovered.

"What happened after Lewis discovered the canyon?" Trinity said.

"The Illuminati found the creatures on their own, so Lewis kept his silence. As it turned out, the Madoc story was a cover. They had fully expected to find some form of intelligent ape or primitive human living in the West, and planned to study and experiment upon them."

"What sorts of experiments?" Trinity asked.

"Blood transfusions, organ transplants, dissections, cross-breeding with the local native population." Ward listed them with the casual indifference of a husband reading his shopping list aloud to the store clerk. "A group of Illuminati remained behind to conduct their experiments, and their names were expunged from the historical record.

"The experiments went nowhere and most of the men abandoned the project after a decade or so. But one man remained behind, a German immigrant named Gebhardt. He had married two native women and sired several children."

"*Two* women?" Trinity scowled. She seemed more offended by that detail than the list of horrible experiments.

"Gebhardt brought his family in on the experiments and the work was passed down through the generations, the family becoming more secretive until only legend remained. That legend made its way to Mister Kane. We discovered the facility. One man was living here alone, trying to continue his family's work, but he lacked the resources to do it well. The research conducted here was primitive, but we gained valuable insights which accelerated our timeline."

"What happened to the man? Did you kill him?" Trinity asked.

"Hardly." Ward laughed. "Last I heard, he is living in Germany with a lovely young wife."

"So, you've resurrected all of the old Illuminati experiments?" Stone asked.

"After a fashion." Ward blanched, hurried on. "But it is more humane. There is no more dissection."

"Are you Illuminati?" Stone asked.

Ward made a small bob of the head.

"How about John Kane?" Trinity said.

Ward barked a laugh. "I am not important enough to have ever met John Kane, much less know his personal affiliations."

"Who is the Worshipful Master?" Stone said quickly, trying to catch the man off guard. He succeeded.

Ward flinched, hesitated. "I don't know." He immediately held up his hands. "I'm telling the truth. He is so far above me in the order I will never know who he is. All I can tell you is John Kane is the butter and egg man, all the money comes from him, but the Worshipful Master calls the shots."

Stone had a suspicion the two were one and the same.

"Did you abduct local women for your experiments?" Trinity demanded.

"The lumber camp acquires patients. I don't ask about

that. I am mostly a bookkeeper," Ward said.

"A man was found beaten to death," Trinity said. "Did your people do that or was it the Bigfoot?"

"I heard about that. He got drunk and wandered into the wrong area. Davis and his men dealt with them."

"Were they responsible for causing the avalanche that nearly killed us?' Stone asked.

"Probably. They have a man who goes around disguised as a Bigfoot and tries to discourage people from going places they shouldn't." Ward didn't quite meet Stone's eye.

"Show us the lab." Stone's words were calm, but inside he was raging.

Ward's face went white as snow. He swayed, gulped, and cleared his throat. "No. I would be signing my own death warrant."

Stone calmly laid his hand on Ward's shoulder. With a sudden movement, he covered Ward's mouth with his other hand, simultaneously digging the tips of his index and middle fingers into the man's trapezius muscle in a spot near the spine. He gave a twist and Ward's eyes bulged and he screamed into Stone's hand. After a count of ten, Stone released the pressure, and Ward's body sagged.

"I don't know how they would kill you," Stone whispered into the man's ear, "but I can promise I will kill you slowly and painfully."

Ward's moment of resolve crumbled. He led them into the main area and up to an old, overstuffed armchair. He tipped it onto its side and the floor underneath it swung up along with it. Down below, a ladder descended to a lower level. From somewhere down below came a low, mournful wail. A woman called out for someone to help her, but her voice was weak and without hope.

"We have to get down there," Trinity said.

"You go first. Then Ward. We'll both be keeping an eye on you," he said to the man.

The shaft they descended was made of hand-cut stone, fitted together with precision. The short hallway they found themselves in was constructed similarly. Bare light bulbs hung from a thick wife, giving off a weak glow.

"The Gebhardt family built this place. They maintained and improved it over the years. We built the space above and expanded on the laboratory beyond this next door.

They watched carefully as Ward removed a key ring from his belt, selected a key, and unlocked the door. He opened it, stepped inside, and beckoned for them to follow.

Stone stepped inside with Trinity hot on his heels. He knew immediately that he had made a mistake. The door slammed shut behind them and everything went black.

INTERLUDE 7

In the ensuing days, Stone's life fell into a pattern. Gideon alternated between attacking, feeding, and instructing him. All of it took place in the darkness. He quickly began to notice changes in himself.

His sense of hearing had been honed to a fine edge. Now, he could hear a single grain of sand fall to the floor. His sense of taste was now refined to the point where he could quickly distinguish which among several buckets of water had a single grain of salt added to it. He sharpened his sense of smell by making him identify ever-fainter scents from increasingly greater distances and enhanced his sense of learning to identify words carved in grains of rice.

He used the latter improved skill to explore his cell. He discovered that the floor was riddled with what felt like trapdoors. That was how Gideon came and went so easily. He took to waiting beside them, hoping to catch Gideon entering, but he always chose the wrong one.

There were also conversations, and not always with Gideon. There were three others—two men, and a woman. Stone eventually could identify them before they spoke, and he named them according to their most identifiable trait: Heavy Walker, Lip Smacker, and Curry Woman.

They engaged Stone in a wide range of discussions,

but all the while they were picking him apart, forcing him to reveal his deepest fears, regrets, and shame. He knew exactly what they were doing, but he was desperate for human interaction, so he opened up in ways he never had before.

Stone was surprised to find the conversations brought him a measure of relief from the heavy burden of guilt he carried. He had never been much of a talker, which had created problems in his personal life. His old girlfriend, Trinity, had called him a 'nut she was determined to crack'. Thinking of her brought back painful memories. Stone had cut her, and all the people he loved, out of his life for their own good.

On one occasion, Curry Woman asks him a rare direct question.

"What finally convinced you to leave the service? Was there a single tipping point?"

Stone took his time before answering. He scratched his chin, reflected on painful memories.

"The decision had been coming for some time. But on my last mission, I came to strongly suspect my commanding officer was working on behalf of the Nazis through a group called the Illuminati. I realized I couldn't know if my marching orders were coming from Washington or Berlin."

There was a long silence before Curry Woman replied.

"Men and institutions are easily corrupted, but values are worth fighting for."

Before Stone could reply, Gideon spoke.

"It is time for a new lesson. Hold out your hand."

As always, Stone could not tell where Gideon was standing. The man sounded like he was everywhere at once. Stone held out his hand and felt something soft land on his palm. It was a single hair. The fact he could feel it was a testament to the progress he had already made.

"Identify it," Gideon said.

"A single hair? Impossible."

A sharp pain burned the back of his calves. He felt it, but after so many days of beatings, his mind barely acknowledged it. It was a dull, distant thing. He threw a punch in the direction he thought the blow had come. He missed and received another whack across the legs for his trouble.

"Identify it."

He drew the hair between his thumb and forefinger. It was thick, coarse. He held it up and sniffed it. He was surprised by its strong odor. Was it just his heightened senses or was there more to it than that? He took another whiff. He didn't think it was a bear. The stench reminded him of a fox's den, or maybe that of a skunk. He was stumped.

"It's a wild animal, but not one I am familiar with." He braced himself, expecting to be hit again. After a few seconds, Gideon spoke.

"You are correct."

After that, there were no more lessons, only beatings.

Stone knew what was happening. They had taught him to see without his eyes. Now it was time to prove he had learned the lesson well enough.

The problem was, even with all his heightened senses, Gideon moved like a cloud of vapor. Only on rare occasions could Stone hear the soft pad of footsteps, or the gentle brush of fabric against flesh. On those occasions, he attacked with fury. One time, his knuckles grazed Gideon's sleeve. He received a cup of coffee along with his

meal that night.
He didn't drink it.
He had a plan.

25- THE FACILITY

Stone heard the sound of running feet. Instinctively he drew his Webley and aimed it toward the noise, but he held his fire. He couldn't say for certain that it was Ward and not Trinity he would be targeting. A moment later he heard a heavy door slam shut.

"You let him get away," Trinity's voice came from the darkness only a few feet away. So it had been Ward running away.

"Did you really think we had no safety measures in place?" Ward called out.

"Keep him talking," Stone whispered softly.

"What did you do?" Trinity added a tremor to her voice, feigning fear.

"The fob on my keyring has a panic button," Ward said. The glee at having turned the tables on them rang brightly in his voice.

Stone crept silently toward the sound of Ward's voice. He had caught only a glimpse of the room before the lights went out. To their left had been a doorway barred by a gate of thick iron bars. Directly ahead was a thick glass door, through which lay a laboratory. Off to the right had been another gated doorway. That was where the voice was coming from.

"What's going to happen?" Trinity said.

"The two of you will be quite useful in our experiments. You are of a healthier stock than the women we have managed to acquire thus far, and Mister Stone is a fine physical specimen, if a bit slow on the uptake."

Stone smirked. He was closing in on Ward. He just needed to avoid notice a bit longer.

"You will not use us like you used those poor people," Trinity said.

"I don't plan on giving you a choice," Ward said with a touch of indifference.

Stone heard a hiss from somewhere up above, caught a whiff of mint. Cool mist drifted down from the ceiling. It was some kind of gas! There was no more time for stealth. He made a dash for Ward.

"If the knockout gas doesn't subdue you, my soldiers will be here shortly."

Stone reached the barred door just as Ward was pushing another button on his key fob. It emitted only the faintest flash of light, but in this utter darkness, it was enough for Stone.

Ward never saw him coming. Stone reached between the bars, grabbed Ward by the collar, and pulled him forward with all his might. Ward struck the bars with a smack. His body went limp and he slid to the floor. The key fob clattered to the ground.

"What's happening?" Trinity shouted.

"Don't breathe the gas. I'm looking for the key fob!"

He took out his IMCO lighter, a refillable metal lighter manufactured in Austria, and flicked it on. A faint circle of yellow light blossomed in the darkness. The mint smell grew stronger. He felt a detached sense of ease, like the effects of nitrous oxide. He needed to hurry.

He finally found the keyring and ran his fingers across

the surface of the fob. There was only a single button.

He clicked it once. Nothing.

Two clicks in quick succession and the lights flickered on. The gas ceased to flow from the ceiling. Across the room, the barred door swung closed seconds before a cadre of beastly men came dashing down the corridor. The Illuminati soldiers. When they reached the barred door, they began to shout incoherently and shake the bars that held them back.

He pointed to the glass door that led to the laboratory and he and Trinity ran inside. Stone sucked in precious breaths of clean, pure air.

Inside, three women lay strapped to hospital beds. A burnt orange liquid dripped from an IV into the women's arms. All three of them looked up in surprise. And off to the left, locked in a cage, a hairy creature huddled with its head between its knees and its large hands covering its head.

"Oh my God," Trinity whispered, "they captured a juvenile Bigfoot."

He and Trinity hurriedly freed the captive women, removed their IVs, and helped them to their feet.

"Who are you?" one of them asked.

"I'm a reporter," Trinity said. "We're here to help you."

"You're not the police? And he doesn't look like any reporter I've ever seen," the woman said, looking at Stone with curiosity.

"He can scarcely write his own name, but he's useful when brute strength is required."

"Take the ladies and make tracks. I'll take care the Bigfoot," Stone said.

"Be careful." Trinity looked nervously at the creature,

which lay slumped against the side of the cage. It was barely four feet tall, but it had muscular arms and sharp teeth. At the sound of Trinity's voice, it lolled its head to the side and gazed at them through glassy eyes.

"I think it's been sedated. I should be okay."

As Trinity ushered the captive women out of the lab and toward the exit, Stone cautiously approached the cage.

"It's all right, pal. I'm going to take you home. Lucky for you I know exactly where you live." He spoke in a soothing voice as he sorted through the keys. The juvenile Bigfoot continued to stare dully at him. When Stone found the correct key and opened its cage, it didn't make a move.

"Moment of truth," Stone said. "I'm going to pick you up. Please don't sink your teeth into my jugular or anything like that." Gingerly, as if picking up a newborn baby, he scooped the creature up, grunting with the effort. The thing weighed as much as a grown man.

They looked at one another for a split second, eyes locking, and Stone saw intelligence and emotion in the creature's eyes.

"It's all right now," he said.

Maybe the Bigfoot understood, because it draped its long arms around his neck and laid its head on his shoulder.

As he left the lab, he took another look around. The Illuminati thugs were struggling to get past the door that held them captive. Stone saw a wildness in their eyes that reminded him of the stories of Viking berserkers.

He had taken two steps into the room when the lights flickered and dimmed. An alarm bell rang. The lights flickered again. A metallic clank echoed through the room. He looked over to see that whatever system held the gate closed had failed. Inch by inch, the thugs were raising the gate.

Stone began to run.

26- THE FIGHT

Stone was halfway up the iron rungs that led to the upper level when the lights went out again. Straining to bear his own weight along with that of the juvenile Bigfoot, his sweaty hand searched for the next rung. He found it, its cold surface icy. It gave a little bit beneath their combined weight.

"Hold on a little bit longer," he mumbled. The young ape let out a groan. "You, too."

In the darkness below he heard shouts and snarls. The Illuminati soldiers were catching up to him. Stone climbed faster. His boots slipped and he nearly fell, but he kept going. The sounds came closer.

He reached for the next rung and his hand closed on empty air. He wobbled and then regained his balance. He had reached the top!

Once out of the shaft, he finally had a free hand to draw his Webley. His first shot missed, but the muzzle flash gave him a glimpse of a giant man, his teeth bared in a bestial grin, scrambling up the rungs with spiderlike agility.

Stone fired again, but the man barely seemed to feel the impact of the .455 slug as it buried itself in his shoulder. His next shot took his target in the eye. He gave a jerk, his body freezing in place as the slug penetrated his brain. His fingers went limp and he fell, taking two of his comrades along with him.

The sudden gunshots had terrified the Bigfoot. It began to howl and flail its arms. It struck the wrist of

Stone's gun hand so hard that his hand went numb. The Webley clattered down into the pit.

"Consarn it!" he swore. "See what you did?"

Without a weapon, he had no choice but to make a run for it. He dashed out into the canyon.

All too soon he heard the Illuminati closing in on him, still howling with bestial rage. Stone had been a track and football star in high school and college, and could outrun most men, but he'd never run a race with a Bigfoot in his arms. As the sounds of pursuit close in, he was forced to accept that he wasn't going to outrun them. He would have to stand and fight.

"I'm gonna rip your arms off!" one of the Illuminati shouted. "I'll eat your..."

A shot rang out and the man let out a roar of pain. And then the forest was filled with flashes of gunfire. More shouts of surprise, pain, and anger behind him. He stole a glance back. A couple of the Illuminati were down, most were bleeding from multiple wounds, but they were still coming. It took a lot to take these men down, if they truly could be considered men anymore.

One of the brutes was almost on top of him. And then a figure came dashing out of the forest. It took him a moment to recognize Constance. She was dressed in snug-fitting clothing and carrying a pistol.

She took aim and squeezed the trigger. Stone winced as the bullet missed him by inches. He heard a sick thud behind him as the slug found its mark. And then Moses burst out of the forest, armed with a shotgun. He opened up with both barrels into the attacking Illuminati.

"Keep going!" Constance shouted. "We'll cover you." Calmly, she raised her pistol and fired again.

As Stone dashed into the shelter of the tree line, he

caught a glimpse of the rest of his rescuers. The shopkeepers, Vince and Deb, along with Harold and Marian Moss. All were armed with hunting rifles and had formed a skirmish line.

When he had reached the shelter of the forest, he stopped and gently laid the young Bigfoot onto the ground. Turning around, he looked for someone to fight, but the battle was coming to an end. The last of the Illuminati soldiers lay on the ground. His shoulders sagged with relief.

"I can't believe you all are here," he said to his rescuers.

"We always knew this canyon was a dark place," Deb said. "It was finally time to take a stand."

"I'm sorry I let you all come here," Moss said. "I swear I didn't know this place was here. I haven't been down into the canyon since the incident."

"You couldn't have stopped us," Stone said. "We are a determined bunch, especially Trinity. Speaking of, where is she?"

"She and Alex are leading the kidnapped women out of the canyon," Moses said. "They were moving slow, so we told them to get a head start."

"Good decision," Stone said.

A shot rang out and he turned to see Constance standing over one of the fallen Illuminati, pistol in her hand. As they watched, she moved to examine another fallen man. She frowned, prodded him with her toe. When he let out a groan, she shot him, too.

"What are you doing?" Stone called.

"Following orders," she said. "I'm with the Bureau of Investigation."

"You knew what was down here and you let us walk

into it unaware?"

"Of course not. The plan was for me to attach myself to Trinity, let her guide me to the facility, assess the situation, and take care of it myself. But Trinity proved to be much more secretive and impetuous than I expected. Once she disappeared, I needed help to find her. After that, things spun out of control."

Stone shook his head. "Using me is one thing, I'm accustomed to it. But you didn't have to make Alex think you cared for him. That was cruel."

Constance hung her head. "I wasn't pretending. I only hope he will forgive me."

"You won't get any help from me," Stone said.

"What exactly is this place?" Vince asked.

Stone described what he had seen and what he had learned from Ward. When he finished, Harold Moss whistled.

"Of all the things my mind could conjure up, I never dreamed of the Illuminati trying to grow Bigfoot-human hybrids."

"The women will need discreet medical attention," Constance said. "And the Bureau will take control of the facility. I cut the solar power line. That will have to be repaired."

"That was your doing?" Stone asked.

"You're welcome," she said.

"The loss of power caused their cage to fail," Stone said, pointing at the fallen Illuminati. "You almost got us all killed."

"My apologies. On the bright side, these were all self-defense killings. Much cleaner than if we were forced to dispose of these men later."

"Do what you like," Stone said, heading back toward

the facility.

"Where are you going?" Constance called out.

"To get my Webley. And then there's one more thing I need to do."

INTERLUDE 8

May, 1927
Five Years Ago

If the usual pattern held, there would be another beating within the hour. He needed to act fast.

He stripped off his clothing and tossed it in the corner where he usually slept. He set the full cup of coffee there, too, and covered it with the overturned bucket that served as his latrine. The coffee aroma needed to be faint. Like coffee breath. Last, he rinsed the smelliest parts of his body using the cup of water provided for his meal.

He selected a spot a few feet away from where his clothing and coffee lay. Close enough that his body odor would be masked by the rich aroma of the drink, but far enough away to temporarily avoid detection.

He waited.

Finally, he heard something. It wasn't much, only the most minuscule intake of breath. He didn't hesitate. He struck with all his might in the direction of the sound.

His fist struck flesh and bone with a satisfying crunch. He had been longing to get back at Gideon for the long hours of abuse. It felt good to even the score a little.

There was a smacking sound like wet meat as Gideon hit the floor. Stone knew at once he had done serious damage.

"Oh, my Lord, Gideon! Did I kill you?"

His hands found the fallen body, and he frowned. His fingers touch soft, smooth flesh. This wasn't Gideon. This person was young and small.

"Cover your eyes, Brock Stone. The light will be blinding."

Stone did as instructed. Even with his hands protecting his shuttered eyelids, he saw a faint red light. Relief flowed through him. Gideon had told him he wasn't blind, but still, it was a comfort to be able to see again.

When he finally opened his eyes, a single candle burned like a sun from a ledge high above. A rope dangled from the ceiling.

Gideon knelt over a young woman with long, black hair and big brown eyes. She sat rubbing her chin and staring balefully at Stone.

"I thought it was you," he said to Gideon.

"This is Dalha. Her name means Moon Goddess. It was her all along."

"You're telling me I've been getting my tail whipped by a teenage girl?"

"I am twenty years old. Well, nearly twenty." Dalha smirked. "At least I am old enough to dress myself."

Stone had forgotten he was naked. He let out a yelp, covered himself, and hurriedly tugged on his filthy clothing.

Dalha laughed. Gideon shook his head.

"Congratulations, Brock Stone," Gideon said. "You have found the first treasure and your new birth is completed. Now you may begin to learn the world anew.

"That's wonderful. Think we could manage my next lesson with a bit less corporal punishment.

"That depends on you." Gideon's eyes twinkled. "Now, you must come with us. Your new life lies on the other side of that door."

27- THE TOMB

Stone's heart was pounding like a bass drum as he carried the juvenile Bigfoot back to its den. The young creature was growing more alert, but still suffered the effects of sedation. It could only walk a few steps before collapsing. There was no way the young ape would ever make it home on its own.

He smelled the Bigfoot before he saw them. The juvenile didn't exactly smell good, but its captors had bathed it and kept it clean. Now the feral smell was overwhelming. They were close by now, watching him.

"If you have any sort of language, I would be much obliged if you would tell your troop that I'm one of the good guys," he said to the juvenile.

As he made his way to the Bigfoot's den, shadows appeared all around him. He wasn't certain if he was being stalked or escorted. He fervently hoped for the latter.

The Bigfoot finally showed themselves when Stone reached the base of the cliff beneath their lair. A male, the dark brown fur of his face sprinkled with white, stepped out in front of Stone. Gently, Stone laid the juvenile on the ground and took a few steps back.

"I'm just bringing him home," Stone said.

The creature stared at him for five gut-wrenching seconds of silence. Then it let out a series of yips like a coyote. Another voice answered. Seconds later a female came scrabbling down the cliff. Her eyes fell on the juvenile and she let out a cry. Still woozy, the young creature crawled to meet her. She picked him up and held him tight.

"Now that we're all back together, I'll just be going." But Stone wasn't going anywhere. The beasts who encircled him didn't move.

The older male bellowed, then tilted his head and twisted his lips to the side. He waited a few seconds, then did it again.

It took Stone a moment to realize that the Bigfoot was pointing with its lips, a practice current among many indigenous tribes around the world. It was pointing up in the direction of the den.

"You want me to go up there?" Stone asked, looking in the direction the beast indicated. The Bigfoot stepped to the side, clearing the way. "That is just… wonderful." He took a breath, remembered something he'd learned from an old friend.

"The beasts are seldom who we think they are." Perhaps it would be all right.

Exhausted and wondering what would happen next, Stone did as he was told. He emerged on a ledge beneath a giant rock overhang. Small cave dwellings pockmarked the rock wall. At least a dozen of the creatures poked their heads out to stare at him.

"It's like Mesa Verde minus the kivas," he said.

The elder male had followed him up. He barked, yipped, and howled at the other beasts, who continued to stare. He turned to Stone and pointed again with his lips, then led the way to a tiny cave in the heart of the dwelling.

Stone was forced to get down and crawl for a good thirty feet before he could stand. He flicked on his IMCO. What he saw took his breath away.

They were inside a cave. Veins of a pale golden-colored alloy streaked the walls. A pyramid six feet tall, made of the same metal, stood before him. Its surface was unmarred. Stone had no way of knowing how old it was, but he had the feeling it was ancient.

On the other side of the pyramid was a stone vault. Three words were carved into the lid.

YMA GORWED MADOC

"It's Welsh," he said. "Here lies Madoc." The legend was true! He could scarcely believe it. "I've got to see this for myself."

Inside lay a skeleton wrapped in moldering furs and homespun fabric. A sword and shield made of the same metal as the pyramid lay upon the dead man's chest. This was Madoc, the legendary prince and explorer.

A scrap of paper was tucked into the fur. Stone carefully removed it. It was dry and brittle, but the cursive writing on it was legible.

Tom, you were right about everything, Madoc, the Orichalcum, the ape men, and the Illuminati. I intend on keeping this secret for as long I live, but if you or our enemies should ever find it, I want it known that I was first.

-ML

Meriwether Lewis. The explorer had successfully completed his mission and had apparently carried the secret to his grave.

Now, the question was, what was Stone going to do about it? He was convinced that the pyramid and the orichalcum were important, and something that needed to be kept away from the Illuminati, and from the government, at least until he had a better understanding of the forces that were at play here.

Madoc wore a fat signet ring made of orichalcum. Stone worked it free and slipped it into his pocket. Once they returned home, he would study it and then decide how much information to share with whom. Until then, he would rely on the Bigfoot to keep the secret. Assuming they would let him leave.

Any fears he had that the beasts might try and hold him captive proved to be unfounded. When he emerged from the cave, only the old male paid him any mind.

The giant beast escorted Stone down the cliff and through the slot canyon back to the trail leading up to Moss family cabin.

"Thank you for trusting me with your secret," Stone said. He thought he understood why the beast had chosen to reveal the cave to him. It was a gift given in gratitude or perhaps repayment for returning their kidnapped child. Maybe the Bigfoot were more human than he had given them credit for.

Trinity was waiting for him at the trailhead. When Stone reached the top, she wrapped her arms around him and held on like a python suffocating its prey.

"What took so long?" she asked. "I was afraid something had happened to you."

"Everything is fine," he said.

Trinity quirked an eyebrow. "You are hiding something."

"What makes you say that?"

"I know you better than anyone in the world. And I will get the story out of you sooner or later. I have my ways." She smiled coyly and planted a soft kiss on his lips.

Stone laughed and held her close, enjoying the feel of her. He nuzzled her soft hair, inhaled her scent. This woman was going to be the death of him. Oddly, he felt just fine about that.

"I look forward to it."

The End

Brock Stone will return in…

"*Indiana Jones* meets *The Rocketeer* in this thrilling, old-school adventure!" Matt James, author of *The Forgotten Future*

A beast out of legend guards a deadly secret!

When investigative reporter Trinity Paige disappears without a trace, Brock Stone embarks on a perilous mission to find her. Deep in the mountains of the Pacific Northwest, the logging town has been beset by disappearances, and the locals lay the blame at the feet of the giant ape man the natives call Sasquatch.

But the dense forests and remote mountain valleys harbor even greater dangers, and the forces of an ancient order will stop at nothing to protect the secret! In order to survive, Brock Stone and his friends must unlock a conspiracy that dates back to the Lewis and Clark expedition!.

This Author's Preferred Edition includes bonus chapters!

PRAISE FOR DAVID WOOD!

"What an adventure! A great read that provides lots of action, and thoughtful insight into strange realms that are sometimes best left unexplored." Paul Kemprecos, author of *Cool Blue Tomb* and the *NUMA Files*

"Excellent pulp adventure in the mold of Doc Savage. Took me back in the best way to books I loved when I was a kid!"- Terry Mixon, author of the *Empire of Bones Saga*

ABOUT THE AUTHOR

David Wood is the USA Today bestselling author of the Dane Maddock Adventures and several other books and series. He also writes fantasy under the pen name David Debord. He's a member of International Thriller Writers and the Horror Writers Association, and also reviews for New York Journal of Books.

Learn more about him and his work at www.davidwoodweb.com or drop by and say hello on Facebook at www.facebook.com/davidwoodbooks.